DISNEY
MALEFICENT
MISTRESS OF EVIL

Adapted by Elizabeth Rudnick

DISNEY PRESS
Los Angeles • New York

Printed in the United States of America
First Hardcover Edition, October 2019
1 3 5 7 9 10 8 6 4 2
FAC-020093-19249

Library of Congress Control Number: 2019940107
ISBN 978-1-368-04560-5

Visit disneybooks.com and disney.com/maleficent

SUSTAINABLE FORESTRY INITIATIVE

Certified Sourcing
www.sfiprogram.org
SFI-00993

Logo Applies to Text Stock Only

For my mother and Jameson, who have taught me
the true meaning of unconditional love

PROLOGUE

THE MOORS WERE QUIET. THE FAERIES WHO CALLED THE LUSH LAND HOME WERE SAFE AND PROTECTED. THEY SPENT THEIR DAYS PLAYING AND LIVING AMONG THE BEAUTIFUL TREES, FLOWERS, AND PLANTS THAT GREW IN ABUNDANCE. They gathered in harmony and danced under the moonlight. They no longer feared the world beyond the borders of the Moors—at least, not as much. They could sleep at night free from nightmares. They were free. They were happy.

Aurora had seen to that.

Five years had passed since Maleficent had bestowed the greatest gift of all on the beautiful young princess. Giving her the kiss of true love, Maleficent had awoken the sleeping beauty and brought her back to rule over the faeries, as had been Aurora's wish. For five years,

Aurora had ruled with grace and kindness. And under her rule, the Moors had thrived.

Maleficent, too, had found peace—as much as the winged fey ever could. She had been a steady presence in Aurora's life and had spent her days happily flying in and around the Moors, watching with pride as Aurora transformed from a young girl to a young woman, from a hesitant princess to a strong queen. She also watched as Aurora and Prince Phillip grew closer, their bond deepening as their love became more real, more mature. Still unsure of humans, Maleficent kept Phillip at a distance. But bit by bit, even his presence had become a familiar—and *almost* welcome—one in the Moors. He spent more time there than in his own kingdom of Ulstead, which lay just across the river.

But where there is light, there is also darkness. And darkness was coming to the Moors. An unexpected evil that was only beginning to reveal itself . . .

CHAPTER ONE

NIGHT HAD FALLEN. INSIDE THE
MOORS, FAERIES SLEPT, LULLED BY THE
TRICKLING WATER OF THE STREAMS
AND THE GENTLE RUSTLE OF THE WIND
THROUGH THE TREES.

Suddenly, the stillness of the night was broken by a
loud snap. Somewhere at the edge of the Moors, a twig
broke.

Three human men, trespassers in the Moors, froze at
the sound. Looking nervously at each other, they waited
to see if the noise had woken anyone—or anything.
When no faeries appeared, they collectively sighed with
relief.

The youngest of the men sighed the loudest. Ben
hadn't wanted to come in the first place. He had heard
the stories of the Moors. He had seen the huge winged
fey who flew in the sky from time to time, and the sight

always unnerved him. He thought the Moors were too close, even with the river separating them from Ulstead. "They can fly," Ben told his family and friends when they teased him about his discomfort with the faeries, "which means they could fly *over* the river if they wanted." It was hard to argue with that logic.

But his friend Colin had told him it would be a quick—and profitable—trip. So he had agreed. Only now he was beginning to regret his decision. From the moment they had entered the Moors, he had been covered in gooseflesh. He knew it was silly, but he felt as though the trees themselves were watching, the grass listening. Even at night, Ulstead was brighter, torches lining the streets and providing illumination in the darkest hour. Here the only light that shone was from the moon and stars hanging in the sky. And that night the sky was dotted with clouds obscuring the little light they had.

"Let's turn back," Ben whispered as Colin and the other man resumed walking.

"And lose good money?" the third man, Thomas, said, shaking his bald head. "Not a chance."

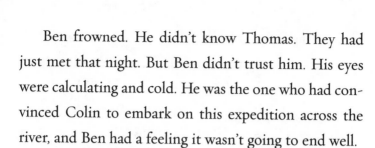

Ben frowned. He didn't know Thomas. They had just met that night. But Ben didn't trust him. His eyes were calculating and cold. He was the one who had convinced Colin to embark on this expedition across the river, and Ben had a feeling it wasn't going to end well.

"Stay close," Colin said, looking over his shoulder at Ben. He didn't say anything more, but he didn't need to. Ben knew that look well enough. Colin was telling him to stay quiet and keep his head down. They both needed the money, no matter the danger.

Reluctantly, Ben followed the men farther into the woods. Deeper in, the sounds were more muffled, the night even darker. Coming to a stop in front of a tall tree, Colin nodded. "Here we are." He pulled a small ax from his pack and began to hack at the trunk of the tree. The sound surprised Ben, and he flinched. Colin kept swinging until, finally, a huge chunk of bark came free. Behind it was a small woodland faerie. The creature was sleeping, slightly snoring, with its little eyes closed. Quickly, Colin reached out, wrapped his hand around the faerie, and stuffed the creature into a bag he had over his shoulder. Colin pulled more bark free and continued to plunder the tree of its faerie occupants. Next to him, Thomas was doing the same, his bald head bent as he focused on his mission.

Ben looked down and saw that the tree was covered in mushrooms. But soon the fungi began to move and squirm, and he realized the toadstools were actually faeries who looked like mushrooms. Taking a deep breath, he reached out and grabbed one.

"*Ow!*" Ben shouted as the mushroom faerie bit him on the finger. The creature was small, his teeth smaller still, so his bite wasn't deadly. But it stung. "You'll pay for that!" Ben said. The faerie bit down again, harder this time. Reflexively, Ben dropped the mushroom faerie, who immediately took off into the woods. Ben followed, exchanging insults with the faerie as they ran. In moments, they had left the thick, muffled stillness of the forest and raced into a clearing. Still shouting insults, Ben plodded into the wide-open space. Out there, he was no longer protected by the shadows of the trees. The other two men had disappeared from view, swallowed up by the forest. But Ben didn't care. He was too focused on getting the faerie into the bag.

He slowed his steps and came to a stop. Like a predator on the hunt, Ben sank to the ground and quieted his breathing. Then he waited. Not hearing footsteps behind him, the mushroom faerie stopped, too. It was only for a moment, but it was just long enough. Shouting, Ben took a diving leap. He flew through the air and then landed on the ground, his hands wrapping tightly around the faerie. As the creature wiggled and squirmed, Ben laughed triumphantly. "I'll get double for a mushroom," he said. "In ya go." Stuffing the faerie deep into the bag, Ben turned. Only then did he realize he was far from where he had started. He headed back toward the woods.

Meanwhile, Colin and Thomas continued to pluck faeries from the tree, oblivious to everything but the task at hand and the visions of money running through their heads. They didn't hear the sound of wings flapping or the gentle rustling of leaves behind them. They didn't realize anything was amiss until, suddenly, the sky went completely black—as if someone had turned off the moon.

Colin looked up and his eyes opened wide. Beside him, Thomas let out a shout. There was a thud as both men dropped their bags, releasing the faeries, who scurried away, murmuring to each other as they ran.

Perched like something out of the men's worst nightmares was Maleficent. Her huge black wings were tucked tight to her back, her green eyes piercing. Her pale skin glowed a brilliant white in stark contrast to the large black horns that rose from her head. As she looked at them, her red lips parted in a smile that sent both men running.

They didn't get far.

Lifting one long, thin finger into the air, Maleficent signaled to the trees. Instantly, they began to bend inward, blocking the men's escape. Branches reached out like arms, grabbing the men and snaking themselves around their limbs as they passed the men from tree to tree until they were once more in front of Maleficent.

This time, the men knew they were trapped.

Slowly, Maleficent approached them. She stopped a short distance away, and her shadow loomed over them both. She said nothing as they squirmed and struggled against their vine-like restraints. "Please," Colin begged.

In response, Maleficent unfurled her wings. They spread, blocking out what little light remained. When stretched, they spanned nearly twelve feet. As terrified as he was, Colin couldn't help being amazed by the wings' obvious strength and undeniable beauty.

She stepped forward, and both men screamed once more.

Ben had just reached the edge of the clearing when the screams started. He leapt as the sound bounced off the trees around him.

Ben didn't hesitate. He didn't know who was screaming—whether it was a faerie or Thomas or Colin. But he didn't care. Every muscle in his body was on alert, and his brain was racing. He had two options— fight or flight. And his body was telling him to run. In an instant, he was off, weaving between the trees as fast as his legs would carry him. His breath came in gasps as he tried to see a path or any familiar landmark that might tell him he was running in the right direction. Seeing none, he plunged forward anyway. A moment later, the trees opened up and he found himself in the middle of a huge field of flowers. They glowed faintly in the night, their red petals open despite the hour. Ben tripped and tumbled into the flowers. He heard snapping as a few of the stems broke. But he didn't care. Not now.

Because ahead, through another grove of trees, he saw the river.

Scrambling to his feet, he ran on, pushing through more flowers and then brushing through the thin trees until he burst onto the riverbank. He jumped into and swam across the river, then clambered onto the shore of Ulstead. He could hear—or so he thought—the faint screams of Colin and Thomas from somewhere across the river. His heart pounding, he made his way up the shore, putting as much distance between himself and the Moors as he could.

Thomas had been vague when he had brought Ben

and Colin into his scheme. All Ben knew was that in exchange for the faeries, they would receive payment. How much and from whom, Thomas did not reveal. Though he had, fortunately, told them where the man lived. Ben followed the streets into the heart of Ulstead and finally stopped in front of a heavy iron door. He lifted his hand and beat on it mercilessly.

A moment later, a slot opened. It was in the middle of the door, about even with Ben's belly button. From behind the slot, two large yellow eyes peered up at him. "I only got one," Ben said, nodding at his bag. When the person behind the door said nothing, Ben shifted nervously on his feet. "But he's a fine specimen."

There was a grumble, which Ben took to mean that he should hand over the bag. He did so, slipping it through the slot. A moment later a wrinkled hand reached out. In the palm were a few scratched coins.

"That's all?" Ben said, surprising himself. "The little 'shroom bit me! Twice!"

Suddenly, the wrinkled hand closed around Ben's belt and tugged—hard. Ben was yanked forward, his face pressed painfully into the door. He winced and pulled his head as far back as he could. He watched as the hand released him and then closed around a flash of red attached to his bag. It was one of the glowing flowers from the Moors. It must have stuck to his bag when he fell. The wrinkled hand snatched the bloom and held it up with reverence. The hand then quickly pulled it inside and, with a snap, slammed the slot shut.

Ben stood there for a long moment, unsure what to do next. Looking at the coins in his hand, he let out a sigh. He had been right. Going to the Moors had not been worth the price. And as he walked to the end of the street and peered back at the woods across the river, he was sure Thomas and Colin would have agreed.

CHAPTER TWO

Aurora stood looking at the roomful of unhappy faeries who had come to confront her. Big, little, thin, plump, they were all aflutter. The air was filled with the sounds of wings and mouths flapping. Aurora listened and watched, her head high, her face calm. Outwardly, she appeared every inch a regal and measured leader. Though in truth, she was actively trying to keep her breaths even and not bite the inside of her lip.

The situation was making her agitated.

For most of the past five years, her rule had been peaceful and relatively painless. There had, of course, been the odd squabble between faeries to sort out. And the occasional dispute between a cranky pixie and a more easygoing mushroom faerie over who had claim to a certain tree. But all in all, it had been rather, well, lovely to be queen of the Moors.

Lately, though, a feeling of unease had begun to filter through her kingdom. Still quiet, beautiful, and relatively peaceful, the Moors weren't in danger, per se. But the feeling was bothering Aurora—and Maleficent. Goddaughter's and godmother's attachment to the land went deep. When the Moors hurt, the two of them hurt, too. Now, as Aurora looked out at the castle full of upset faeries, she realized it was beginning to bother the Moor folk as well.

Lifting her head, she focused on the gathered faeries. She knew they were waiting for her to continue. The weekly update had become a tradition of sorts. Aurora felt that an informed kingdom was a happy kingdom. Although some days, like today, were more frustrating than others. "Next item of business," she said, "the missing faeries. I've sent another clan of tree-sprites to search the backwoods. They'll report back to me at nightfall." Beside her she heard Lief mutter. She turned her gaze at the large tree faerie, who served as one of her top advisors.

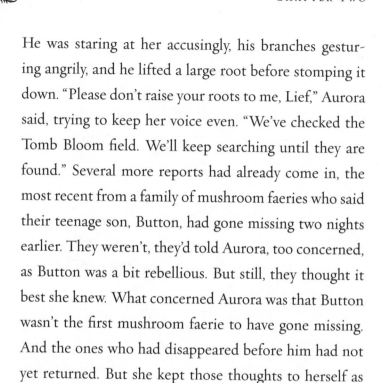

He was staring at her accusingly, his branches gesturing angrily, and he lifted a large root before stomping it down. "Please don't raise your roots to me, Lief," Aurora said, trying to keep her voice even. "We've checked the Tomb Bloom field. We'll keep searching until they are found." Several more reports had already come in, the most recent from a family of mushroom faeries who said their teenage son, Button, had gone missing two nights earlier. They weren't, they'd told Aurora, too concerned, as Button was a bit rebellious. But still, they thought it best she knew. What concerned Aurora was that Button wasn't the first mushroom faerie to have gone missing. And the ones who had disappeared before him had not yet returned. But she kept those thoughts to herself as she doled out words of comfort.

Lief was not satisfied by Aurora's response. Again he waved his branch-like hands in the air. This time, the movement caused a few leaves to flutter free and fall to the ground in front of Aurora.

"Yes, I'm aware the farmers from Ulstead have been using our river water," she answered.

Lief bellowed.

Aurora raised an eyebrow at the faerie's reaction. She relied on Lief to be calm and steady, and this was completely out of character for him. She pressed on, ignoring her advisor's growing agitation. "I've decided it's time for our kingdoms to start working together." She paused. "For peace."

But a loud caw interrupted her. Looking toward it, Aurora saw Diaval perched on a branch. The raven's feathers were ruffled and she could see judgment in his black eyes. She held back a groan. Diaval was supposed to be on her side. He was supposed to be *her* friend.

Stepping away from Lief and out of Diaval's line of sight, Aurora addressed the faeries. She knew that they were upset and that they thought humans were to blame for the disappearances of their friends and family. She also knew that it was up to her to reassure them even if she didn't have any answers—yet. "I am queen of the Moors and I am human," she said.

Instantly the room grew quiet. Sighing, Aurora moved toward her throne and sat down. The large chair was made of soft leaves and green grasses. It rose out of the natural floor of her castle and seemed to embrace her as she sat. Two flower faeries rushed to her sides and began braiding her hair. "I realize it's been an adjustment," Aurora went on, "but the borders were opened for a reason. In time, you will get used to the occasional human. You just need to give them a chance—the same chance you gave me."

Her words were met with mixed reactions. Some of the faeries shifted their feet. Others fluttered their wings faster. A few even whispered among themselves. But no one made a move to leave. "What is going on here today?" Aurora said, becoming exasperated. She was standing now, and her voice was a bit stronger. "In case you didn't know, I *live* here!" *And this castle has gotten entirely too crowded,* she added silently. "Everyone, please, wait outside!"

Flopping back into her throne, Aurora exhaled as she watched the faeries file out of the room. To her dismay, they didn't continue walking and leave the palace. Instead, they lined up right beyond the door, eager

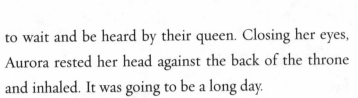

to wait and be heard by their queen. Closing her eyes, Aurora rested her head against the back of the throne and inhaled. It was going to be a long day.

"A word, Your Majesty?"

Opening one eye, Aurora saw Flittle hovering in front of her. The small pixie looked the same as she had the day Aurora had met her years earlier. Her curly brown hair, the ends tipped with blue that matched her dress, bounced as she fluttered nervously. Even when Aurora had been a young girl, Flittle had been flighty and prone to bouts of nervousness. She was acting even more anxious than usual. Hovering beside Flittle were Thistlewit and Knotgrass. Together, the three pixies were looking at her with odd expressions. She loved them. After all, they had raised her—for the most part. But that day she wasn't sure she could tolerate their antics.

"Pixies," she chastised, "you need to wait your turn like everybody else."

"This can't wait, Your Grace," Knotgrass said, shaking her head. She brushed her hands over her simple red dress. "We know you'll want to see this!"

Flittle nodded. "We could hardly believe our luck," she said.

Holding out her hand, Knotgrass revealed a tiny spiked ball.

Aurora sat up. "Is that—"

Before she could finish, the "ball" transformed into a hedgehog faerie.

"Pinto!" Aurora said, clapping her hands together happily at the sight of her sweet and wonderful friend. The little hedgehog faerie often disappeared for weeks at a time, and it warmed Aurora's heart to see her now. Perhaps the day was taking a turn for the better.

"She has come bearing gifts," Flittle explained. "The first sap from the warming trees."

"It's for the big day!" Thistlewit blurted out.

Aurora cocked her head. "What big day?" she asked. She saw Flittle give the little blond pixie a hard nudge with her elbow.

Just then, Pinto leapt onto the arm of the throne and raced toward the top. Reaching out, the hedgehog faerie grabbed the delicate crown off Aurora's head, and

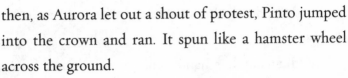

then, as Aurora let out a shout of protest, Pinto jumped into the crown and ran. It spun like a hamster wheel across the ground.

"Pinto!" Aurora said, leaping to her feet and giving chase as the faerie darted away. "I'm not in the mood for that!" Just when she thought the day couldn't get more exhausting . . .

Ignoring Aurora, Pinto kept going. She ran out of the throne room, down the halls, out of the castle, and into the Moors beyond. Aurora followed, her hands clenched in tight fists as she muttered under her breath. Usually, she liked to walk slowly through her kingdom, taking in the lush beauty and saying hello to the various faeries she passed. But not that day. She ignored their greetings and didn't even notice how bright the sun was shining or that the sky was a brilliant blue. Instead, she kept her eyes glued on Pinto.

Reaching the edge of a small lake, Pinto hesitated. It was just long enough for Aurora to reach her. Leaning down, she grabbed for Pinto—and her crown. "Got you!" she started to say. But as she spoke, her foot slipped on the muddy ground and she fell forward, landing in the water with a splash.

"What has gotten into all of you?" Aurora yelled, pushing herself to her feet. She roughly brushed off the mud and water that covered the front of her dress. Her feet were drenched in muck. As she brushed a strand of hair out of her face, she felt a line of dirt follow her finger. As Aurora looked at the three pixies, her eyes narrowed. She usually enjoyed a fun game of tag or hide-and-seek in the Moors. But not that day.

"Well, since you asked . . ." Thistlewit began. But before she could finish, Knotgrass slammed her into the mud, smooshing her face down and turning her green dress brown.

Aurora gasped. The pixies were known for picking on each other. She couldn't count the times she had woken up to their squabbling when they had lived in their small forest cottage. But this? It was downright ridiculous.

"There she goes, Your Majesty!" Flittle exclaimed.

Aurora turned and saw Pinto. The faerie had grabbed

hold of the crown again and was running it toward a large weeping willow. Aurora followed.

Pulling back the long branches that fell to the ground, Aurora stepped inside. Behind her, the branches dropped, and Aurora suddenly found herself in silence. The soft green leaves muffled the noise from outside and enclosed her in a canopy with the sunlight dappling through. The space was warm and inviting.

"Pinto!" Aurora called, her voice sounding loud in the silence. "Come out here now."

When no hedgehog faerie appeared, Aurora moved farther into the natural room. In the center, on a rock near the trunk of the willow, she saw her crown. Aurora picked it up and held it in her hand. So much fuss for a thing that was merely a symbol. She hadn't even really wanted a crown when Maleficent first made her queen of the Moors. But she had given in when presented with the beautiful headpiece made of the branches of her kingdom. Staring at the royal symbol, Aurora realized that so much of her life was about compromise, ruling, and helping her subjects. In the silence beneath the willow tree, she noted that it had been days since she had been truly alone.

Just then, she heard a soft rustling. Aurora turned, expecting to see Pinto. But to her surprise, she found herself looking at Phillip. Even now, five years after they had met, he made her feel weak in the knees and undeniably, indescribably happy. Usually.

"Phillip!" she said. "I'm so happy you're here." *Although I wish I weren't in such a state,* she added silently, keenly aware of her mud-covered clothing.

The prince moved closer. A lock of his brown hair fell over his eyes, and Aurora resisted the urge to reach out and brush it back. She was always telling him teasingly that for a prince, he was remarkably relaxed about his grooming. But secretly she loved the touch of wildness about him. "And I you," he said, his voice sounding oddly shaky. "Of course. Since I'm the one who came here. To see you."

Aurora smiled but her eyes continued to roam the area, searching for Pinto. True, seeing Phillip was a pleasant surprise, but with the Moors turned to madness and a castle full of complainants, she didn't have the time to spend with him or to wonder why he was acting strange. She had work to do. The peace she had promised moments earlier could only be made with action—and she could not bring action if she was searching all over for a wayward hedgehog faerie.

Still scanning the ground for Pinto, Aurora decided to do both at once. "I wanted to ask you something. Do you think there could be a union? Between Ulstead and the Moors?"

"A union," Phillip repeated, his voice catching in his throat. "Do I—"

Aurora cut him off. "Yes. I've been imagining a bridge. To connect the two lands."

"Oh, a bridge," Phillip said, once again repeating her words. "Yes, a bridge is a wonderful idea."

"Oh, good. I'm so glad," she said as she finally turned her full attention to the prince. Then her eyes narrowed and she cocked her head. She had been so caught up in her own drama that she had failed to really look at him when he had appeared. But there was something about Phillip's presence—and his outfit—that gave her pause. "Wait," she finally said, "that's your formal coat."

As her heart began to beat faster, she looked around. The willow tree. The warm, romantic canopy. The pixies' odd behavior and Pinto's race through the woods. Phillip in his formal coat . . . He was going to propose!

She bit the inside of her cheek to keep in the squeal she wanted to let out. "You're in on all of this, aren't you?" she said, her voice trembling. She wiped at her dress, wishing she hadn't taken the tumble into the water.

"If you're busy, I could always . . ." Phillip started, his voice teasing.

"No!" Aurora said, shaking her head. "Not busy at all."

"Because I'd hate to take up your precious time. . . ."

Aurora wanted to hit herself upside the head. Why had she gone on and on about her stupid day? "All ears," she said, smiling encouragingly. "What did you want to talk about?"

Phillip stepped closer. The smile on his face faded and he grew serious, his eyes full of emotion. The world seemed to slow as he stopped in front of her. "Five years ago, I thought I lost you forever," he said. He took her hand and squeezed it gently. Both of them remembered when she had nearly died and what they had almost lost. Opening her palm, he gently ran a fingertip up her finger, stopping at the dark red scar that would forever be a reminder of when she had pricked her finger on the magic spindle. When he looked up, Phillip met Aurora's gaze. "I've decided to reclaim this day for us. I have loved you since the moment I met you. . . ."

If she had had any doubt that this was a proposal, it vanished. Aurora's eyes filled with tears. "I can't believe this is happening," she whispered.

Phillip laughed lightly, bringing levity to the serious moment. "I haven't even got to the good part yet."

"I think it's pretty good," Aurora said softly.

Phillip reached into the pocket of his coat and pulled

out a small box. "There is no magic, and no curse, that can ever keep me away from you, Aurora." He paused, and then, his eyes filling with light and love, he teased, "Are you sure this is a good time? I could probably . . ." Aurora shook her head, and Phillip kneeled down. "Will you marry me?"

The words were barely out of his mouth before Aurora let out a loud "Yes!"

"Yes?" Phillip asked, though her answer had been perfectly clear.

Tears of joy falling down her cheeks, Aurora nodded. "Just stand up and kiss me," she said.

Phillip didn't need to be told twice. Rising to his feet, he pulled Aurora to him, and as his lips closed over hers, the willow tree exploded into a riot of brilliant colors. Flower faeries, having waited patiently for Aurora's response, flew into the air in celebration. Aurora didn't even notice, lost in the kiss—and in the love she felt for Phillip. She hadn't known, until the moment he asked, how very deep and true that love was. They had been through so much together. And now they had the rest of their lives for many more adventures.

Hearing sniffles, Aurora finally pulled free of the kiss. Looking toward the sound, she laughed as she saw the three pixies hovering in the air. Knotgrass's cheeks were stained with tears of joy as she clasped her hands. "We're having a wedding!" she cried.

Beside Aurora, Phillip nodded. But then his expression turned serious. "Of course, we have to tell our parents."

Suddenly, the warm and fuzzy feeling that had been flooding Aurora's body dimmed. She imagined the look on Maleficent's face and shivered. "Do we?" she asked. As if on cue, there was a loud caw. Looking up, she saw a large black raven take flight from a nearby branch. Diaval. The bird was no doubt flying to tell Maleficent the news. He had always been the Dark Fey's eyes and ears.

Even so, Aurora knew she would have to tell Maleficent the news herself—eventually. While it was tempting to hide in the canopy of the willow tree forever, she took Phillip's hand in hers, and they headed back to her castle. She would use their walk to prepare herself for what Maleficent might say. She had a feeling it wouldn't be "congratulations."

CHAPTER THREE

MALEFICENT STOOD ATOP THE HIGH CRAG. THE SHEER, FOREBODING ROCK MONOLITH WAS THE HIGHEST POINT IN THE MOORS. FROM IT, MALEFICENT COULD LOOK OUT OVER THE ENTIRE KINGDOM. Although she was welcome in Aurora's castle, she was more comfortable here. On the crag, she was alone and free from the incessant chatter of the other faeries.

As the only one of her kind, Maleficent had never had the camaraderie that came with growing up among others like oneself. She did not understand the faeries' need to constantly check in with one another or tell each other about their days. She preferred her solitude. And if she was being honest, she knew that most of the faerie folk were fine with that. She had earned her reputation as a strong and fierce Dark Fey the hard way—through war and violence. Even now, years after peace had come to the Moors, that reputation hung over her. Her presence still often made the smaller, more lighthearted faeries nervous.

In truth, the only one she had not grown tired of was Aurora. The girl, who was more daughter than friend, never ceased to amaze Maleficent. She was never bored with or weary of her. When she was around Aurora, she never felt uncomfortable or self-conscious about the huge wings and dark horns that were hers alone. Maleficent could spend hours with her, wandering the Moors, delighting in how the girl still found such joy in every corner of the kingdom. The love that had grown between them was stronger than ever, and it was made even greater by all they had overcome. It seemed there was nothing that could break their bond.

Hearing the familiar sound of flapping wings, Maleficent waited as Diaval, her trusted raven and companion, landed behind her. He squawked.

"What?" she asked. She twirled her hand, and a small flicker of green magic flew out, transforming Diaval from bird to human.

Maleficent raised an eyebrow. The man looked terrified. He was often skittish and a little bit flighty—an effect of spending more than half his life in bird form. But the fear she saw now was unusual.

"Mistress," he began, "I, uh, I bring some news." He stopped and took a few quick breaths. "But before I say this news, you need to promise you won't . . . execute me."

Maleficent sneered, revealing her perfectly white teeth and the pair of small fangs that made even her nicest smile seem menacing. She knew that there were those in the Moors who believed she had gone soft when she made a human their queen. But most knew better. They knew that while Maleficent loved Aurora, she was still a Dark Fey. And no one doubted the damage Maleficent could—and would—inflict on the fools who dared try threaten her. "Tell me," she said, losing patience with Diaval, "or you'll wish I had."

Gulping, Diaval went on. "It's nothing of consequence, really, no reason to overreact." He paused, realizing his voice sounded as shaky as he felt. He had known Maleficent far too long. There was no chance

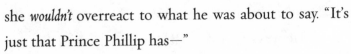

she *wouldn't* overreact to what he was about to say. "It's just that Prince Phillip has—"

"Leprosy?" Maleficent interjected hopefully.

"No, mistress," Diaval said, shaking his head. He tried again. "Phillip has—"

"Black plague? Yellow fever?" Maleficent asked.

"Mistress," Diaval said, growing exasperated. His next words came out in a rush. "Prince Phillip has asked Aurora—and here's the part where I'm going to remind you not to kill me—asked her if she will become his . . ."

Maleficent's face somehow became even paler. It turned out there *was* something that could get between her and Aurora: Phillip.

As Maleficent lifted her head, her green eyes bored into Diaval. "Don't ruin my morning," she warned.

Around them, the wind picked up—slowly at first, but then it whirled faster and faster. The air crackled with electricity. The sky turned darker as Maleficent spread her wings. A storm was brewing. Then, without another word, she took off into the air.

Diaval shivered as he watched her go. "You're taking

this incredibly well!" he shouted. A moment later, there was a flash of green as he transformed back into a bird and followed her into the sky.

Phillip couldn't stop smiling. Aurora had said yes! For days he had been nervously planning and thinking, worrying and hoping. And now it was over, and everything had gone perfectly. Well, except for the whole part when she fell into the pond. But still. She had said yes. She had said yes even before he could properly ask. And they were going to spend the rest of their lives together. He thought his smile couldn't possibly get wider, but then it did.

Phillip's horse galloped through the main gates of Ulstead, and he rode toward the castle. It loomed large, its huge white facade sparkling in the sun. The two towers that dominated the building rose high into the sky, their tips appearing to vanish into the clouds. Everything about Castle Ulstead was big, lavish, and ornate. The village that lay at its feet mirrored the wealth of the castle in its own way. The buildings were smaller and their sides were more muted than the blinding white of the castle, but they were strong and well built. The roads Phillip's horse now cantered over were smooth, and the people he passed looked healthy and happy.

Phillip slowed his horse to a walk when he spotted Percival waiting for him in the town square. He and Percival had grown up together and remained friends— despite the fact that Phillip was a prince and Percival was now a general in Phillip's father's army.

"So, tell me, sire," Percival said when Phillip arrived. "Will I be the best man? Or did you choose a filthy creature from the Moors?"

Phillip's eyes darted toward his friend. The young general did nothing to hide his hatred of the Moors and any creature that made the place its home. Despite his open, kind face, Percival had a dark and angry streak when it came to the Moors. Phillip could usually just ignore the man's opinion, but every now and then, Percival said or did something that crossed the line. In those moments, Phillip did his best to keep his mouth shut and his hands by his sides. But every so often

Percival found himself at the end of Phillip's sword and would, for a good length of time after, be sure to temper his tone.

"General," Phillip said now, trying to keep the conversation on lighter—happier—ground, "if you're asking if she said yes—"

Percival cut him off. "Oh, I know she said yes," he said. "What human wouldn't want to escape that place?"

"What do you have against the Moor folk, Percival?" Phillip asked. He was not in the mood for Percival's sour attitude. Not that day. Not on the day of his engagement to the woman he loved, who ruled over those very folk Percival showed such hatred for.

Percival didn't answer right away. Instead, he scowled and kicked his horse's sides. It was time to go. Together the two men moved through the square and toward the castle. "Moor *folk*?" Percival repeated. "Is that what we call winged beasts and murderous trees?"

Phillip frowned and gave Percival a warning look. "You mind your tongue, General," he said. "You know nothing about them." Percival's opinion was based on tales and adventures he had not participated in. He had not been part of King Stefan's battle. He had not been there to witness the atrocities committed by the *humans* against the faeries. Yet like many others, Percival believed that the exaggerated stories were true—and that evil lay outside the human heart instead of within it. To him, Maleficent was a monster.

Percival went on. "I know Maleficent is a killer of men. Destroyed half an army by herself—"

"She's not like that, General," Phillip said, coming to the defense of the Dark Fey. He almost smiled. His future mother-in-law, if that was what he could call her, would have laughed at hearing him defend her. She barely acknowledged him when they did interact. And when she did, it was usually to ask if he was feeling well—with the obvious hope he wasn't.

"It's my job to protect this kingdom," Percival went on. "And I'll do so, old friend—without hesitation." Once again, he kicked his horse and galloped forward, leaving Phillip to follow. Behind him, Phillip sighed, some of his earlier happiness fading. He and Aurora were sure of their love for each other. They had spent hours daydreaming about uniting their kingdoms and showing both faerie and human that they could coexist. But the road to that unity was going to be bumpy. Phillip knew Percival wasn't the only one who wouldn't be happy about his engagement.

Clucking at his horse, Phillip trotted toward the castle and his parents with butterflies in his stomach. They, too, were sure to have strong reactions to his news.

King John longed to stretch. He had been sitting for hours on his throne under the weight of his ornate coat and heavy crown. At his wife's request, a fur blanket—with the animal's head still attached—was draped over him. And he held a long scepter. The throne, uncomfortable on a good day, felt like it was stabbing into his backside after hours and hours of posing for his royal portrait.

But he would do what he must to make his wife happy.

Noticing movement from the corner of his eye, King

John smiled—but only slightly. He had already been reprimanded enough by the artist. "Ingrith," he said in greeting. "You're the only one I can trust. Be honest—how do I look?"

The queen stepped farther into the dark room. Even without light to illuminate her skin, it glowed the same color as the moon. Her dress clung to her body, accentuating her thin frame, and her blond hair, nearly white, was pulled back tight to her scalp. Her eyes, as she scanned the canvas, were cold. It was she, not the king, who looked like a piece of art. A cold stone statue.

"Like the greatest king in the history of Ulstead," she finally said, her tone flat.

The king either didn't notice the tone or chose to ignore it. "And see your place of honor," he went on, apparently pleased with his wife's response. "Right beside me."

Unable to move his head, he couldn't see the grimace that contorted the queen's objectively beautiful face. Nor did he notice as her hands clenched at her sides and she took a sharp breath. When she spoke, however, her voice was even and calm. "And that's where I'll always be."

Ingrith despised that as queen, she was always seen as second to her weak and ineffectual husband. Just the sight of the man made her feel ill. When he spoke, his words full of flowery nonsense and foolish romantic notions, she wanted to put her hands over her ears and scream. Theirs was not a love match. It had been a match of convenience. The chances Ingrith would adore him had been slim and the silly stuff of John's favorite fairy tales. But at least she could have married someone she admired. Or even *liked*. Instead, she had married a man whose constant declarations of love and adoration made her skin crawl.

But the kingdom—and her husband—expected her to be the doting wife. So she was. She smiled for portraits. She forged alliances, instigated wars, and expanded their rule while John talked endlessly about impossible peace and waxed poetic with his son about the power of love.

She did it for one reason, and one reason alone: she

needed John and the power his title and her marriage had brought. So let others believe he was the leader. Let the kingdom believe that she had no agenda, that John was the reason they lived under such prosperity. They would soon discover how wrong they were.

Hearing the doors open once again, Queen Ingrith turned, happy for an excuse to stop looking at her husband. Gerda, the royal engineer, walked in briskly, carrying a large crate. She was one of the few members of the royal court who was not intimidated by Queen Ingrith. Gerda had been part of the court for years and provided the king with wisdom, advice, and, when asked, weaponry. But she was, at heart, loyal to the queen.

Stopping in front of the royal pair, Gerda nodded. Leaning down, she placed the crate on the ground in front of them. It was filled to the brim, the wooden sides strained by its contents. "Your Majesty," Gerda said, addressing the king, "spoils from the annexation of the Midlands have arrived." She pointed to the top of the pile. "Weapons."

King John shook his head, earning himself a sharp

glare from the portrait artist. "We have no need for arms," he said. "Our days of war are over."

The queen bit the inside of her cheek. Her husband was a fool. There would always be war. It was part of running a kingdom. If there wasn't war outside, there was war inside. If there were not enemies far away, there were enemies at the gate. Or in their case, across the river. But John had always seen the world through the eyes of a child, naive and hopeful. He believed war should be a last resort. Ingrith thought otherwise.

She reached into the pile and pulled out a crossbow. While the weapons Gerda had acquired were antique, they still worked. Lifting it, she cocked the bow, holding the weapon with practiced ease. "One can never be too careful," she said, turning so that the bow was aimed right at the king.

Gerda watched the queen, her expression blank but her eyes curious. "Your Majesty, it's cocked," she warned.

There was a tense moment as Gerda looked at the queen, and the queen looked at the king. "Is it, now?" Ingrith asked, feigning ignorance. She tossed the bow to

Gerda, who caught it. When she did, the weapon fired. The arrow flew wildly through the air and slammed into a statue next to the doorway.

"You need to be more careful," Ingrith said, eyeing the quivering arrow.

Gerda nodded, taking the blame as expected. As she went to retrieve the arrow, Ingrith moved farther into the room. Bright beams of sunlight poured through the windows at the back, illuminating the gray tiled floor and making it shine. Ingrith sidestepped the light, avoiding it as if it were a puddle of mud.

The doors to the throne room opened again. Her expression turned happy—or rather, less cold—when she saw her son. Phillip's handsome face was full of joy as he strode toward his parents.

"Father, Mother . . ." he began.

"Well?" King John said, standing up. He didn't even care that the moment he stood, the artist began to mutter under his breath. "What did she say?" the king pressed him.

Phillip's smile broadened. "She said yes!"

"That's marvelous news!" King John said, throwing his arms around his son. "Two kingdoms will finally be one!"

Ingrith looked at the two men as they embraced—one old and foolish, the other young and reckless. She should have known Phillip would go to his father for advice about his relationship with Aurora. The boy had never sought her out for heart-to-heart conversations. Lessons on strategy and war were more her cup of tea. But she couldn't blame him. After all, she had never hidden her feelings about Aurora. She just wished her oaf of a husband had warned her that a betrothal was imminent.

Pulling free from his father's hug, Phillip turned to Ingrith. "Mother," Phillip began, doubt creeping into his voice, "I know this goes against your wishes. But if you'll spend some time with Aurora . . ."

Mother and son shared a look and an awkward silence.

If I had had a heads-up, I could have planned this better, Ingrith thought, wishing, yet again, that her husband wasn't completely incompetent. But she knew she needed to say something to her son. Finally, she nodded. "Yes," she said, trying to keep her tone soft. "Perhaps I've been selfish, looking at this the wrong way. I owe you and Aurora an apology."

"Mother?" Phillip said, not hiding his surprise at her response.

"You've made your choice," she went on, surprising him still further, "so now is a time to celebrate." She walked to him, and she, too, hugged him. The gesture felt foreign to her. She couldn't remember the last time she had embraced her son. But the moment seemed to call for it.

In her arms, Phillip stood awkwardly. "I'm glad you finally approve," he said.

"Much more than that," Ingrith said, pulling back. Her mind had begun to race. A delightfully wicked idea had just come to her. She had been seeing this all wrong. The union wasn't a problem. It was a *solution*. She could use it to further a plan she had hatched years earlier. Because of circumstance and position, she had been unable to do more than plot. That had changed. Phillip's engagement had handed her an opportunity on a silver platter. She couldn't, however, let Phillip have any inkling that she had anything but the best of intentions. She needed him to *believe* that she was behind his marriage—disgusting as she found it. If he remained in the dark, she would be able to right the wrongs from the past and bring her life's goal to fruition—an end to the faerie folk once and for all. Pulling her lips back in a smile, she went on. "I'm ready to welcome your fiancée with open arms. Why don't we have her over for dinner?"

Phillip looked shocked. But he smiled. "That would be incredible," he said.

"But under one condition," Ingrith added, causing Phillip's smile to momentarily falter. "She will bring her godmother."

The room became silent. Ingrith had known her statement would bring such a reaction. She had never—not once in the five years Aurora had been in her son's life—set foot in the Moors. Nor had she opened her doors to the girl or Maleficent. She had also never made her feelings toward the faeries secret. All who knew her knew of her disdain. And now she was inviting the queen of the Moors and the girl's Dark Fey godmother to dinner?

"We will meet the one who raised her," she went on. "Right here in this castle."

Unaware of what his wife was really plotting, King John clapped his hands together happily. "The queen is right," he said.

"I'm not sure her godmother will—" Phillip started.

But Ingrith stopped him. Lifting a pale thin hand in the air, she shook her head. "But I insist," she said. "After all, we will soon be family. There is no other way."

"The queen is right," King John repeated. "Let it be known throughout the kingdom: My son is going to marry Aurora. And Maleficent is coming to Ulstead."

As the king returned to his portrait, Ingrith kept a smile plastered on her face. It was just like John to take her decree and make it his own. She let him . . . for the moment. Soon enough he wouldn't be her problem.

But first she had a dinner to plan. A few ideas had already come to mind. First course: polite conversation. Dessert: a hearty helping of Maleficent humble pie. And then, finally, destruction of the Moors—and every last faerie who called that disgusting forest home.

CHAPTER FOUR

Until that moment, Aurora had never realized she could feel simultaneously wonderful and terrible. She was dreading the conversation she knew she was about to have with Maleficent. It made her stomach ache.

But back outside Aurora's castle, the weather was oblivious to her inner turmoil. The sun was shining; the brilliant blue sky was unmarred by a single cloud. And for the first time in days, there were no faeries waiting on her to solve a dispute or bring light to an issue that had no solution. The only sounds were the soft breeze that sang through the trees and the voices of Knotgrass, Flittle, and Thistlewit. The three pixies were, as usual, bickering among themselves. Aurora slowed her pacing and a smile tugged at her lips. Their voices brought back many good memories—as well as a few she would rather leave behind. The pixies had been her only role models for the long years she had lived hidden in the cottage in the forest. Their voices were as familiar to her as her own, and as familiar as Maleficent's. They had scolded her and praised her. They had raised her and guided her, just as Maleficent had.

Thinking of the Dark Fey, Aurora took a breath and resumed pacing. She fiddled with the ring that now adorned her left hand. The sight of it filled her with a happiness she could not describe. But when she raised her gaze to the sky, waiting for her godmother, that feeling faded and was replaced by trepidation.

She loved Maleficent. She loved her biting comments that were harsh because she cared. She loved the fey's hard scowls that hid her soft heart. She loved Maleficent for all the reasons some feared her. But she also loved her because she was her mother. Maybe not biologically, but that had never mattered. Still, despite the strength of their relationship, Aurora found herself jittery as she waited for Maleficent to arrive. She had seen Diaval flying away from the willow tree after the proposal. It was only a matter of time.

As if on cue, the sky darkened as Maleficent swooped in front of the sun's rays. Behind her was Diaval, struggling to keep up with the fey's anger-fueled speed. A great gust of wind kicked up as the Dark Fey descended to the ground, her wide wings thrumming in the air. Knotgrass and the other pixies grabbed for a tree, trying to stay upright.

Landing in front of Aurora, Maleficent drew her wings to her back. Diaval flew to a nearby branch and settled on it nervously. The air around Aurora seemed to thicken as dark clouds rolled across the Moors. Maleficent's emotions had always been tied to the Moors' landscape. It was easy to see she was not pleased.

"Hello, Aurora," Maleficent said, stepping closer. Her thick red lips glistened and her green eyes narrowed as she looked down at Aurora. Behind the fey, a small pond began to boil. "Anything . . . new?" The words oozed from her mouth.

Aurora took a deep breath. There had been times before when she and her godmother had not seen eye to eye. And they had made their way back together. They would do so again—she hoped. "Godmother," she said, "Phillip asked me to marry him."

"Poor thing," Maleficent said, the tone of her voice implying she cared very little for him despite the words. "How'd he take it?"

"My answer is yes," Aurora said, the words coming out in a rush.

"And mine is . . . no," Maleficent countered.

Aurora lifted her head. Even though she had grown taller and stronger—and had become queen—she still felt small beside her godmother. Nevertheless, this was important—as important as the safety of the moors she ruled over. And if her godmother had taught her one thing, it was to stand behind her convictions. Putting on a brave face, she pulled her shoulders back. Then she spoke her mind. "I wasn't really asking."

"Nor was I," Maleficent said, unbothered by her goddaughter's bravado.

Aurora held back a groan. She had known Maleficent was going to be difficult, but this was ridiculous. She was acting like Knotgrass when Flittle turned everything in the cottage blue one summer—including Knotgrass's favorite dress. "What's next?" Aurora said, her voice sounding precariously close to a whine. "You'll turn him into a goat? Disembowel him?"

Maleficent shrugged. "It's a start."

This time, Aurora held in a scream. Phillip had never done anything to Maleficent! He had, in fact, bent over backward to prove himself to the faerie time and time again. Aurora would have thought that if nothing else, his attempt to save her life years ago would have meant *something* to Maleficent. But despite all Phillip had done, Maleficent remained wary of him and his intentions.

As if reading her mind, Maleficent paced slowly around the young queen. Her long fingers curled over the top of her wooden staff, and her dark eyebrows rose on her pale face. "Are you aware there are faeries miss-ing in the Moors?" she asked accusingly.

"Of course," Aurora said, annoyed that on top

of everything, her godmother would assume she was unaware of what was happening in her kingdom. She had heard the rumors. She had reassured the families of the missing faeries. She would get to the bottom of it. It was just taking time. But Aurora was most upset that Maleficent would bring that up in a conversation about Phillip. "What does this have to do with him?" she asked.

Maleficent nodded, the implication clear. She believed humans to be the cause of the disappearances. "Last I checked," Maleficent went on, "he was human, a repellent, loathsome—"

"I'm a human," Aurora said, cutting her off.

"And I've never held that against you."

Aurora shook her head and cast her eyes downward. "Until I fell in love," she said. Sadness filled Aurora's face. Her godmother was wrong. Maleficent *had* held Aurora's humanness against her before. Aurora couldn't help remembering another time, long, long before, when Maleficent had cursed her—simply for being the daughter of the human who had broken the Dark Fey's heart. Did Maleficent not see that she was punishing Aurora once again, for doing exactly what Maleficent herself had done? How was Aurora any different than Maleficent had been as a girl? True, Maleficent's love story had ended in heartbreak. But ultimately, the story had brought Aurora and Maleficent together. True love had saved them both.

Around them, the woods grew quiet. Aurora and Maleficent looked at each other, a million words unspoken between them. Aurora saw a flash of pain on her godmother's face and felt a flicker of uncertainty. Was the pain for Aurora or for herself? The silence stretched on as the Dark Fey seemed to lose herself in a memory. Aurora didn't need to ask what Maleficent was thinking about. She knew. It was the same thing she had just been thinking about. Maleficent was remembering Aurora's father, King Stefan, and his betrayal.

"True love doesn't always end well, beastie," Maleficent said, the pet name making Aurora smile despite the tears that suddenly welled up in her eyes.

"I'm asking you to trust me," Aurora said. "Let

Phillip and me prove you wrong." She moved closer to Maleficent, forcing the faerie to stop pacing. "The king and queen are celebrating tonight. They've invited us both to the castle."

Maleficent's eyes widened. "You want me . . . to meet . . . his parents?" Nothing could have shocked her more.

Up on his branch, Diaval cawed in disbelief.

"It's just dinner," Aurora said, though she knew it was much more than that.

Her large black horns sweeping back and forth as she shook her head, Maleficent curled her lips. "They don't want me in Ulstead," she pointed out. "Why would I agree?"

"Because his mother wishes to meet mine."

The words hung heavy in the air. Maleficent did not say anything as Aurora stared up at her with eyes full of hope. Then Maleficent turned to go.

Reflexively, Aurora took a step closer, her arm outstretched, as if she was going to try to stop her godmother. But then Aurora lowered her arm. She knew there was no point in forcing Maleficent to stay. "Just think about it," she added. "For me."

Maleficent's answer was a flap of her wings as she lifted into the sky. Aurora watched her until she was nothing but a black dot on the horizon. With a troubled heart, Aurora turned and headed into her castle. She would have to hope that somewhere, deep inside, Maleficent could find it in her to accept Phillip and his family. Because if she couldn't . . . Aurora shook her head. She couldn't think about that now. The pending dinner was worrisome enough.

Phillip stood inside the royal chambers, deep within the walls of Castle Ulstead. As a boy, he had loved coming to the grand rooms, listening from the wings as his father negotiated with foreign dignitaries or met with his war council to plan attacks. The lavish oversized furnishings had seemed huge to him; the large animal heads mounted on the wall always seemed to follow him magically. He had always been simultaneously terrified and intrigued by the trophies his mother insisted King

John keep in the chambers. This had been an exotic and foreign place. The lack of life—both literal and metaphorical—had always made him both excited and uncomfortable.

As Phillip got older, however, the intrigue had faded. Now he found the lifeless eyes of the animals depressing. And while he still enjoyed spending time with his father, he often wished they could do it outside, away from the room that, despite its size and ever-present fire, seemed to suffocate him and make him feel cold to his core.

Unaware of his son's dark thoughts, King John strode across the room. He wore a huge grin, and in his hand he had a sword. "I want you to wear this tonight," he said, holding it out.

"The king's sword?" Phillip gingerly reached out and took it. The weapon felt surprisingly light. He had seen it strapped to his father's side hundreds of times, and in his head it had always been a heavy, unwieldy weapon. The significance of his father's giving it to him now was not lost on Phillip. But the king seemed to feel the moment needed explanation.

"Because of you," he said, his voice full of pride, "Ulstead and the Moors will be united at last."

Phillip shook his head, trying to hand the sword back. "My love for Aurora has nothing to do with politics," he protested.

"Your love will ensure peace for generations," King John said, changing the sentiment ever so slightly but enough to make it clear he understood. Then his eyes welled with tears. Phillip struggled not to smile. His father was nothing if not a romantic. He should have known that to King John, the marriage was a love match first and foremost. The king pushed the sword into Phillip's hand once more and added, "I've never been more proud."

Phillip slowly holstered the sword, shifting on his feet as he got used to the weight of the object at his hip. Then he looked back at his father. He had come to the royal chambers for a reason and been distracted. He needed to talk about his mother. Before she had composed herself, Phillip had seen a flash of anger cross her face when she first heard his news, and it had been eating at him. Phillip had come to his father now because he had always done so when he was worried about something. "What about Mother?" he finally asked. "Is she upset?"

"She'll learn to love who you love," the king answered without hesitation. Then, clapping a hand on Phillip's back, he began to tell him a story about when his and Ingrith's betrothal had been announced.

Phillip only half listened. He hoped his father was right. But a piece of him wished that his mother didn't have to *learn* to love Aurora. He didn't expect her to love Aurora in the unconditional way he did. But why was it so hard for her to embrace Aurora when everyone else did with such joy and ease? Was Ingrith incapable—or simply unwilling?

CHAPTER FIVE

STANDING IN THE SHADOWS OF THE ROYAL CHAMBERS, QUEEN INGRITH HAD WATCHED AND LISTENED AS HER HUSBAND AND SON BLATHERED ON ABOUT LOVE AND UNITY. She had been glad that her face was hidden. At least the two men could not see her eyes as they rolled or the small grimace she bore when she heard she would grow to love Aurora in time. All the time in the world would not be enough. To her, Aurora was only a pawn in a game of chess she had been secretly playing for years.

Having heard more than she had wished, Ingrith slipped through the shadows into the sanctity of her dressing room. The space was off-limits to John and, for the most part, any of the castle staff. Besides a few very trusted maids, she kept the room empty of visitors, which was how she liked it. Walking into the center of the room, she exhaled deeply. This place calmed her. On either side, the walls were lined with lavish gowns of gray, silver, white, and black. Not one for color, she found the monochrome effect settling. Diamonds and other precious gems sat upon the shelves, and dozens upon dozens of shoes were paired together on a wall of their own. Against the far wall were several dress forms made to her exact measurements. The most fragile and lovely of her gowns adorned them.

Ingrith held out a hand as she walked toward them. But instead of gently running her fingers over the delicate lace on one, she pushed against it. The dress form tilted back until there was a quiet click. Behind the form, a door slid open, revealing stairs that led down into darkness.

The queen allowed herself the smallest of smiles. This was the real reason she loved her dressing chambers and did not allow anyone in. Or rather, the door *led* to the reason she kept her private rooms private.

Sliding by the dress form, Ingrith slipped through the door and began to descend the staircase. Her footfalls echoed off the stone walls as she went deeper and deeper. Every few feet, a sconce illuminated the stairway, revealing ancient stone that was always damp and cold. But Ingrith didn't need the light to know where she was going. She had made this journey more times than she could possibly count.

As she approached the bottom of the stairs, the space grew lighter and she could hear water bubbling. Every once in a while, a clink sounded, as though something was hitting against glass. Finally, she arrived at a landing. Ingrith stepped forward and into a huge cavernous space. The arched ceilings rose nearly fifteen feet, and several stone bridges dissected the room, revealing an even larger room below. Ingrith walked to it and peered down.

Her reaction was the same as it always was when she looked upon her laboratory: a mixture of pleasure and pride. She had spent years making the space into what it was now. Every piece of gleaming equipment had been handpicked. Every specimen was there at her orders. Every experiment was done at her request. Her eyes narrowed as she scanned the room for Lickspittle. Spotting the pixie hunched over a workbench, she made her way to him.

He didn't hear her at first. His big yellow eyes were focused on the microscope in front of him. Long, thin fingers were wrapped around the black tube that led to the lenses. As he gazed into the eyepiece, his fingers tightened and loosened, reminding Ingrith of a spider making a web. Lickspittle's skin, which had once been smooth and the color of moonlight, had long since turned to a spongy yellow. It was mottled with spots and scars earned in various mishaps in the lab over the years. Even his clothes had taken on the same yellowish hue. The apron he wore over his chest was stained, and its large pocket was full of various equipment—none of which looked particularly clean. Ingrith hated how dirty Lickspittle appeared. But she tried to ignore it. After

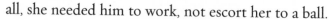
all, she needed him to work, not escort her to a ball.

Lickspittle was the only other soul who knew of Ingrith's lab. Captured years earlier by Ingrith, he had lost his wings—and his soul—and become her lead experimenter. He seemed to have forgotten over the years that he was even a pixie at all. He often referred to himself as though he were a human, and Ingrith had stopped correcting him. It served her purposes better if the creature did not feel any connection to the faeries and pixies he worked on in the name of science. Or rather, in the name of Ingrith. Without an ounce of remorse, he spent his days and nights hidden in the bowels of Castle Ulstead, performing crude trials on his own kind.

He lifted his head from the microscope, and donning a pair of safety glasses, he turned his big yellow eyes to a glowing red flower. He hummed as he continued to work, tapping the center of the flower over a dish, causing a gold powder to float down. The beautiful flower seemed out of place in the darkness of the room and in the spongy hands of Lickspittle. All around him were dozens of glass jars, and inside them were trapped faeries of every shape and size. This was where the Moors' faeries had been disappearing to—all by Ingrith's order.

Hearing Ingrith's footfalls, Lickspittle finally looked up. He blinked his eyes rapidly as he bowed. "Your Majesty," he said.

"You need to move faster, Lickspittle," the queen replied, not bothering with pleasantries. She hesitated and quickly looked at the flower before moving toward a nook in the back of the lab.

Inside, the floor was piled high with all manner of mythical relics. More items had been placed carefully and intentionally on shelves that stuck out from the walls. There were wooden bowls filled with dusty objects long since rotted to unrecognizable, jars labeled "unicorn tears" and "Pegasus teeth," and even what appeared to be the skull of a dragon. It was like walking into a museum of mysterious objects from all over the world, all remnants of a long-ago time when people believed in myth and magic. In the heart of the nook, separated from the other pieces, was Ingrith's most prized possession. She had tracked down the item nearly five years earlier and secreted it away to the lab. Even now, in the dark and dank laboratory, it appeared to shine with untapped magic. She stepped closer, her eyes locked on the spinning wheel.

Behind her, Lickspittle appeared. Following her gaze, he shook his head. "I've never understood your search for a spinning wheel, Your Majesty," he said.

Ingrith didn't turn her head, her eyes still focused on the wheel. "It's the only treasure I'll ever need," she said. In time, Lickspittle would understand. In time, *everyone* would understand.

Maleficent had spent a good part of the afternoon at the cottage that had once been Aurora's home. When Aurora had become queen of the Moors, it was abandoned and taken over by weeds and wildflowers that grew up through the floor and wrapped around the decaying furniture. Dust covered what bare surfaces remained, and when beams of sunlight made it through the dirty windows, they caught and illuminated the specks that floated in the air.

Despite the state of the cottage, it still felt comforting. A nod to Aurora's time there, perhaps, and the love she had put into the house and everything she did. Standing beside the window to Aurora's room, Maleficent looked at the small cradle that still sat in the far corner. Her breath caught in her throat as she remembered watching the little girl slumber, her tiny hands tightening and loosening on the soft piece of fabric she had carried with her everywhere. She remembered how Aurora's nose twitched in her sleep, as though she were smelling something delightful. And how she always woke up smiling. Even as a child, Aurora had found the good in everything and everyone—including Maleficent.

Maleficent couldn't let the girl down—even if it meant going to Castle Ulstead and dining with the enemy.

Maleficent flew away from the cottage and returned to Aurora's castle. Summoning Diaval, she made her way to a small reflecting pond. For the past hour now, she had been practicing her smile.

Pulling back her lips for the hundredth time, she turned to Diaval. In his human form, he stood a safe distance away. He had learned that when Maleficent asked for feedback, she rarely took it well. "And now with slightly less fang," he suggested.

"How's this?" Maleficent asked, lifting her upper lip so that it perched awkwardly over her fangs.

Diaval shook his head. "Mistress, I can smile nicer," he said, "and I have a beak." Maleficent raised her hand, her fingers twitching, to turn the infuriating man back into a silent bird. But before she could, Diaval stopped her. "Wait," he cried, attempting to save himself. "Try the greeting again."

Maleficent sighed but lowered her finger. Diaval was right to push her. Although she had no desire to go to this dinner, she wasn't doing it for herself—she was doing it for Aurora. And that meant playing the part, down to the smiles and forced hellos. Maleficent took a deep breath, then tried again as she nodded ever so slightly. "How kind of you to invite me this evening," she said, her voice sounding grating even to her own ears.

"Remember," Diaval said, "not a threat."

Maleficent nodded and tried again. She thought of every sickly-sweet nice thing she had ever heard Aurora say. She thought of the way the young girl's voice always became a bit higher when she was trying to reassure Maleficent she was okay. Channeling Aurora, Maleficent said, "How kind of you to invite me this evening," her voice now creepily nice.

"Better," Diaval said. "And now the curtsy."

Maleficent was done. She didn't even have to raise her finger to make Diaval step back. She had had enough. This was as polished as she would ever be. It was time for a break.

Diaval sensed her frustration, and his face softened. "She loves that boy very much," he said gently. "You're doing her a great kindness."

Maleficent opened her mouth, a snide retort on the tip of her tongue, but she stopped herself when Aurora came into view. Wearing a simple gown of the lightest pink that brushed the ground, its neckline dipping ever so slightly and with no added adornment, she looked every inch the elegant queen. A few flowers were tucked into the top half of her hair, which was pulled back, accentuating her large eyes and blushing cheeks. The rest of her long blond locks hung free and swayed in the gentle breeze that blew through the clearing.

"Lovely," Diaval said when Maleficent remained silent.

Aurora smiled at her old friend and then moved to stand in front of Maleficent. She was holding something. "I have something for you," she said. Lifting her hands, Aurora revealed a long black scarf. The fabric was plain, but rich and heavy, the same fabric as Maleficent's dress. "It's . . . for your horns." She paused, smiling nervously. "I just thought it might make Phillip's family feel more comfortable."

That stung.

Maleficent inhaled sharply. It was a natural reflex, honed by those years, long before, when she had thought her horns a source of shame. It had been a while since she had felt the need to hide who she was from others. The thought made her feel sick and angry at the same time. Her expression must have made her thoughts clear, because Aurora immediately looked contrite.

"And you as well," she said. "But maybe it's a bad idea. . . ."

Diaval's reminder of how much Aurora loved Phillip echoed back to Maleficent, and she saw, in a flash, the cradle in the cottage. Aurora had only ever asked for Maleficent's love. It had taken Maleficent years to realize how much the girl meant to her and years more to grow comfortable with that love. If Aurora had taught her anything, it was that kindness could be found in the smallest of gestures. Slowly, she reached out and took the fabric from Aurora.

"Thank you," the girl said, relieved.

Maleficent nodded. "Come on, then," she said. "Let's get this over with."

She turned and strode out of the clearing and into the heart of the Moors. She heard Aurora and Diaval

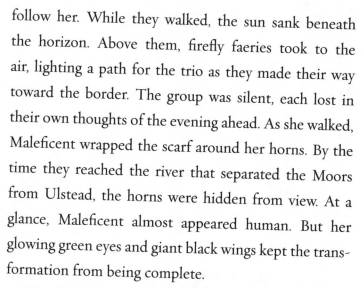

follow her. While they walked, the sun sank beneath the horizon. Above them, firefly faeries took to the air, lighting a path for the trio as they made their way toward the border. The group was silent, each lost in their own thoughts of the evening ahead. As she walked, Maleficent wrapped the scarf around her horns. By the time they reached the river that separated the Moors from Ulstead, the horns were hidden from view. At a glance, Maleficent almost appeared human. But her glowing green eyes and giant black wings kept the transformation from being complete.

Reaching the river that connected the two kingdoms, Maleficent hesitated. This was the farthest she had been from the Moors in a long, long time. Looking out over the water, she saw the lights of the village come on one by one. From where she stood, they almost looked like the firefly faeries that twinkled above them. But Maleficent knew better. She knew that for every light that came on, there was a human. And where there were humans, there was distrust—and iron.

Taking a deep breath, Maleficent pressed on. With

a wave of her hand, a bridge made of flowers and vines appeared. She stepped forward, the others following. While every inch of Maleficent wanted to turn back or take to the skies and fly away, she knew she could not. Looking over her shoulder, she saw Aurora, whose face was aglow with the anticipation of seeing Phillip.

No, Maleficent had to do this.

It took only a few moments to reach the village that sat at the foot of Castle Ulstead. As they walked onto the main street, they heard shutters slamming. A few villagers lingered on the street, holding torches in front of them menacingly. But aside from them, the village appeared to be mostly deserted.

"Such a warm welcome," Maleficent said, raising an eyebrow as she looked around.

"In fairness, you waged war on the last human kingdom you visited," Diaval pointed out.

Maleficent shrugged. She couldn't argue with that. Continuing, they passed a group of young boys and girls. They were staring at the trio, mouths open and eyes wide. Flashing them a smile—complete with fangs—Maleficent bit back a laugh as they squealed and ran away. It was just too easy. Human children were such easily frightened creatures.

Finally, the trio arrived at the main gate. As they passed through a soaring archway, Maleficent took note of the soldiers who stood at attention. For a kingdom at peace, they certainly seemed prepared for war. Shooting them a look, Maleficent strode forward. But she was forced to a halt when Castle Ulstead came into full view.

The castle was massive. The tips of its tallest towers soared high into the sky, and everything around it was oversized as well. As they moved inside, huge topiaries lining the entryway depicted a menagerie of wild and tame animals. Wolves stood cowering beneath the hooves of horses; elephants reared up beside barking dogs. Maleficent couldn't help thinking it was grotesque. Baring a fang, she moved on. There were nearly a dozen suits of armor, each one exaggerated in size. No actual human could ever have worn them; they stood only as symbols. And hanging from the ceiling was a chandelier that dripped with jewels and the wax from a thousand candles.

As they proceeded down the entry hall, Maleficent shuddered. Beside the iron shields and weapons that lined the walls, huge paintings were hung, depicting scenes of man against nature. A king on a hunt, his hounds chasing a frightened deer. Another king and his dozens of soldiers killing a huge bear. Farther on, a gigantic tapestry spanned nearly twenty feet, depicting Saint George violently slaying a dragon.

"Would you ever consider changing me into a bear?" Diaval asked, dragging Maleficent's attention from the art. His voice, while soft, still echoed under the high ceilings. "I think I'd make a rather impressive bear. Have you ever seen their claws?"

Maleficent shot him a look. "Why are you talking about bears?" she asked, annoyed. Then she saw that his face had paled and he looked as shaken as she felt. She grinned slightly as she realized she knew the answer. "You're trying to distract me."

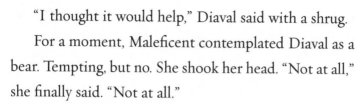

"I thought it would help," Diaval said with a shrug.

For a moment, Maleficent contemplated Diaval as a bear. Tempting, but no. She shook her head. "Not at all," she finally said. "Not at all."

Diaval was still laughing as they reached the doors to the main hall. But his laughter died as the massive doors pulled open. Standing on the other side were Phillip and his parents.

"Presenting . . . Queen Aurora of the Moors!" Gerda announced.

Maleficent glanced out the corner of her eye at Aurora. She loved the girl. But the cost seemed high. Were her horns just another price she would have to pay to make Aurora happy and appease the human king and queen? Taking a deep breath, she lifted her head. It really would be so much better if this were a nightmare and she could simply open her eyes and wake up.

But there was no turning back now. The king and queen were not the village children. They would not be scared off by a sneer. She was going to have to put on a show and hope that the whole night played out quickly.

Unless she managed to feel "sick." She looked at Diaval. Why hadn't she thought of that sooner? Taking a breath, she looked ahead. She would have to remember that for the next time she was forced to make nice with Phillip's parents. That is, if there was a next time. . . .

CHAPTER SIX

AURORA'S HEART WAS POUNDING. IN ALL HER YEARS WITH PHILLIP, SHE HAD NEVER MET HIS PARENTS OR BEEN TO HIS CASTLE. SHE HAD NEVER THOUGHT IT STRANGE . . . UNTIL NOW. Standing in the doorway, she felt small and provincial. Everything about the Ulstead palace, king, and queen screamed "opulence" and "elegance." She ran a hand nervously down her dress and wondered briefly if she should have worn something else.

But then Phillip stepped forward, a huge smile on his face, and all of Aurora's doubts melted away. It didn't matter where he lived; he loved her. *That* was all that mattered.

"Aurora," he said, taking her hands and lowering his head so only she could hear him. "Am I glad to see you."

Smiling up at him, Aurora squeezed his hands. "I

can't believe you grew up here," she whispered. "It's beautiful."

"It's just like any home . . . with fifty-seven bedrooms," he said, laughing. His laughter settled her nerves. True, his home was bigger than her entire kingdom, but that didn't change who he was. And at least he could laugh at the absurdity of it all. Aurora felt her love for Phillip deepen.

Holding her hand reassuringly, Phillip straightened up and turned so that he and Aurora were facing his parents—together. King John, taking that as his cue, stepped forward. Immediately, the king pulled her into a huge hug. "Aurora," he said, his voice warm. "It is truly an honor. Welcome to Ulstead."

Aurora couldn't help smiling back at Phillip's father. He was a smaller, rounder version of his son with an almost childish sweetness to him. "The pleasure is mine, Your Majesty," she said.

Pulling free, she turned as the queen stepped forward. She felt a flash of nerves as she took in the beautiful older woman. In the light from the candles on the wall, Queen Ingrith's cheekbones were sharp and her eyes cold. Her dress, silver with hundreds of gems, sparkled and made Aurora once again feel plain. But then the woman smiled and held out her hand. "Such a beautiful girl," she said, her voice soft. "I can see how you stole Phillip's heart."

As Aurora moved to take her hand, the queen sneezed. Aurora stepped back, startled.

"The flowers in your hair," Queen Ingrith said, covering her nose. "I'm allergic."

"I'm so sorry, Your Majesty," Aurora quickly said, lifting a hand self-consciously to her head. She had forgotten that Phillip had mentioned his mother was, as he'd put it, allergic to everything. But before she could say anything else, she heard footfalls.

"Presenting," Gerda said loudly, "Maleficent."

A moment later, Maleficent entered the room. Her powerful wings dragged on the floor behind her as she strode forward. Her face was unreadable. Diaval followed, his own face an open book as he anxiously took in the surroundings.

"Hello, Maleficent," Phillip said, moving forward. "It is wonderful to see you again." Aurora looked at him, silently thanking him. She knew that this moment was tense for him, too. But he was, as always, handling it like a gentleman. Gesturing to his parents, he went on. "This is my father, King John of Ulstead. And my mother, Queen Ingrith."

"Welcome to our home," King John said warmly.

Maleficent didn't move. Aurora held her breath as she watched her godmother lock eyes with Queen Ingrith. There was a long beat during which Aurora was sure something terrible would happen. And then, to her surprise, Maleficent bowed her head ever so slightly. "How kind of you to invite me this evening," she said. Aurora nearly fainted in relief and mouthed a small thank-you to Diaval. She knew he was responsible for that.

Unaware of any tension, King John smiled broadly. "I trust you had no trouble finding the castle."

Maleficent caught Diaval's eyes. Aurora knew exactly what it meant. Clearly, Diaval's guidance had only gotten them through the first hello, not the small talk. Turning back to the king, Maleficent raised an eyebrow. "Why?" she asked. "Would I?"

Diaval jumped in, trying to save the moment. "No trouble at all."

"This is Diaval," Aurora said, introducing her friend, since no one else had. She didn't bother to mention that he was actually a raven in human form. She figured that was something they could address later.

Queen Ingrith nodded. "Thank you for coming," she said. "Please, make yourself at home."

Just then, the sound of a bell rang out and a servant announced that dinner was served. Breathing a sigh of relief, Aurora followed the king and queen as they made their way down the hall. Maleficent had survived the introductions. Now they just had to eat dinner. How hard could that be?

Candles lit an immense table in the middle of an equally massive dining room. In the corner, a group of musicians quietly played as servants hurried about, loading the table with food and drink. Despite the dozens of candles and heavy drapes that lined the windows, the room felt oddly cold. Aurora got the impression it was too big to ever be warm.

Aurora followed Gerda to her spot and took a seat next to Diaval. The engineer gently pushed her in, then stepped back and moved to stand beside Percival. Aurora nodded at the soldier, whom she had only met on occasion but had heard plenty about from Phillip. The young man looked anxious, his face drawing into a frown as he returned her nod.

Across from her, Phillip and his parents were ushered into their seats as well. While she felt uncomfortable with the formality, the royal family looked completely at ease. *They probably eat like this every night,* Aurora thought before she turned to watch Maleficent approach the table. The chair meant for her was ornate, complete with a high back and heavy armrests. Aurora realized there was no way Maleficent would be able to sit in it with her wings. Luckily, Diaval had come to the same conclusion and, jumping to his feet, found a stool to replace the chair. Nodding to him, Maleficent sat, folding her huge black wings behind her. The tops of her wings towered behind her, making it appear as if she were sitting on a black throne even taller than those of King John and Queen Ingrith.

As Maleficent settled herself, a huge cat, Arabella, lumbered over. Eyeing Diaval, she climbed onto her own chair and began to groom herself.

A moment later, the servants set gold dishes in front of the guests. Aurora looked down, impressed. She had known this was an important dinner, but she hadn't expected such fine treatment. Then again, given what she had seen of the castle thus far, perhaps this was just regular royal treatment. Lifting her goblet, also made of gold, to her lips, Aurora sipped as she took in the rest of the table. Everything was opulent, from the golden plates and candlesticks to the multiple pieces of silverware. The servants then ushered out an impossible amount of food, all covered with metallic domes. But while the table was full, Aurora noticed it lacked any flowers or natural decoration. Whenever she held a dinner in the Moors, her table was full of flowers.

Satisfied that everyone was ready, Ingrith slowly removed the lid of the first dish. On it was a whole game hen. Aurora swallowed nervously as she looked to Maleficent for her reaction.

"Roasted bird," the Dark Fey said. "Delicious."

Beside her, a servant put a game hen in front of Diaval. The man stared at in horror, and Aurora felt a wave of sympathy. There was no way Diaval would eat a bird. He *was* a bird. But to Maleficent's credit, she was trying. Aurora watched her godmother reach for her fork. But as soon as Maleficent's fingers touched the utensil, she gasped and dropped it back to the table.

"Maleficent?" Queen Ingrith asked. "Is there a problem?"

"Iron," Maleficent said simply.

Aurora shifted in her seat. "Majesty, as you are sensitive to nature, she is averse to iron," she explained as gently as possible.

"I had no idea! Take it away at once!" Queen Ingrith said to a hovering servant. While she appeared apologetic, there was something unsympathetic in her voice. Then she looked back at Maleficent. "I'm allergic to all forms of nature," she explained. "Even a ray of sunshine can harm my skin."

King John took a huge bite of his own bird, swallowed, and then laughed. "Have you ever met someone who prefers the darkness?" he asked, trying to make a joke. "Is awake all hours of the night?"

"Yes," Maleficent said flatly. "Bats."

Ingrith's eyes narrowed at the jab. "I trust you'll be comfortable using your hands?" Her tone was light, but Ingrith clearly meant to insult Maleficent with the remark. The Dark Fey was, after all, not exactly human.

Aurora glanced at Phillip. Their eyes met, and she silently pleaded with him to do something. Reading the look easily, Phillip tried to change the subject. "Such a warm spell of weather," he said.

"It certainly is!" Aurora said, her voice sounding overly eager even to her own ears.

King John seemed oblivious to it all. He clinked his fork against his goblet. Because the glass was made of solid gold, it made more of a thud than a clink. But the noise got everyone's attention. "We'd like to offer a small gift to Phillip and Aurora—to celebrate their glorious future together." At his signal, a servant wheeled in a huge ornate solid-gold baby cradle and placed it in the middle of the room. "Ingrith chose it herself."

Aurora and Maleficent stared at the cradle for a long moment, each one of them thinking the same thing: it wasn't right for a baby. Cradles were meant to be comforting and cozy. What kind of baby could be soothed in something like that?

"It's . . . lovely," Aurora finally said, finding her voice and her manners first.

Ingrith looked pleased. "I simply can't wait to have a little one running through the castle again," she said.

Aurora tried not to look surprised. While Phillip had never said a bad word about his mother, he had never said anything overly warm, either. On more than one occasion, he had implied that he was far closer to his father because his mother had been distant. Aurora had a hard time imagining Ingrith chasing after a young Phillip. In fact, she couldn't imagine it at all. But the statement was also upsetting. She and Phillip had never spoken of children. After all, they had only just gotten engaged. Plus she assumed any child would be raised in the Moors; that was her home.

It seemed Maleficent agreed. Dragging her eyes from the golden cradle, she turned her cold stare to Ingrith. "*This* castle?" she said.

Ingrith nodded. "Of course," she answered, her tone as icy as Maleficent's stare. "This will be their home."

Maleficent looked at Aurora. She raised a perfectly arched brow as if to say, *Oh, really?*

But before Aurora could respond, King John bumbled on. "We hear Aurora has a castle of her own," he said.

"Yes, I'm curious," Ingrith added. "How *did* Aurora become queen of the Moors?"

Maleficent picked up the most harmless-looking item on her plate—a lone stalk of asparagus—and bit

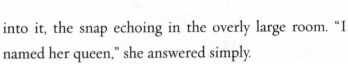

into it, the snap echoing in the overly large room. "I named her queen," she answered simply.

"Her castle is quite stunning," Phillip said, looking at his parents. "You must see it." Aurora wanted to hug him. He was trying so hard to keep the conversation light.

But Ingrith was after something, and she wouldn't be deterred. "But in fact," she went on, "she has another castle, does she not?"

"Mother," Phillip warned.

Ingrith brushed him off. "There's one on the Moors—and one left behind by her father. King . . . Stefan, was it?"

At the mention of the man's name, both Aurora and Maleficent bristled. Taking a deep breath, Aurora tried to calm her racing heart. She wasn't sure why Phillip's mother felt the need to bring up the past, but she was not going to let it ruin the present. Taking the high road, she nodded and said, "That castle was never my home. It was given to the people."

"So you're also a true princess," Ingrith said, pressing

on, "even though Stefan died—or was he killed? Remind me, did he die or was he killed?"

Any warmth that had crept into the room over the earlier part of the dinner evaporated. Seeing Aurora's rosy cheeks lose some of their color, Maleficent frowned. "Both," she snapped.

The room grew silent. Ingrith's eyes were locked on Maleficent, while Maleficent's were glued to her goddaughter. Aurora, meanwhile, just looked at her lap, willing her tears not to fall. She hated thinking of that night years ago. She had been given so much— Maleficent's love, the Moors, Phillip—but the cost had been high. On a night that was supposed to be about the future, she was miserable thinking about the past.

"Because I remember the story of a baby," Ingrith continued. "A baby cursed to sleep and never wake up." As she spoke, her eyes remained fixed on Maleficent. It was clear the queen knew there was more to the story. But how much more did she know?

Oblivious, King John put a hand to his heart. "Now, who would do such a thing to an innocent child?" he asked, sounding truly horrified. Aurora would have smiled had she not been so upset. He really had no idea what was going on.

But Maleficent did. "There are many who prey on the innocent," she said, "as I'm sure your kind would agree."

"My kind?" Ingrith said. "You mean *humans*?"

Aurora had had enough. Looking up, she tried to put a stop to the conversation once and for all. "Shall we listen to the music?" she suggested. At the same time, Phillip raised a hand, signaling for another round of drinks.

But there was nothing they could do. The conversation would not be stopped.

"We have faeries missing from the Moors," Maleficent said, "stolen by human poachers."

"This is the first I've heard of it," King John said, looking truly surprised.

Maleficent lifted her pale, thin shoulders in the faintest of shrugs.

In a flash, Ingrith latched on to the Dark Fey's gesture.

Ingrith had been hoping for something like this to happen. There was glee in her eyes and excitement in her voice when she spoke. "It sounds as if you're accusing His Majesty," she said, feigning concern.

"Someone gave the order," Maleficent retorted.

Instantly, Ingrith was on her feet, pointing at Maleficent. "How dare you accuse the king!"

The table erupted in voices. As Phillip rushed to Maleficent's defense, the king wondered aloud why anyone would bother to steal a faerie. Ingrith, meanwhile, continued with her accusations. The only two who did not speak were Aurora and Maleficent, but the looks they exchanged spoke volumes.

Percival stepped forward and cleared his throat, earning the attention of the diners. Aurora turned. She knew him only from the stories Phillip had told her. But she did not like what she sensed. Her suspicions were confirmed when he finally spoke. "Your Majesty," he said, addressing King John, "I must report two peasants were found dead just outside the Moors. They had been missing for several days."

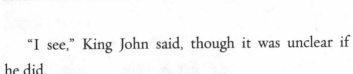

"I see," King John said, though it was unclear if he did.

But Ingrith jumped at the news. "Yes, we *all* see," she said. "The borders are open, but humans are not welcome! Isn't that right?"

Aurora had listened for long enough. She had tried to brush off the conversation about her father. She had tried to pretend the cradle was not a thinly veiled power play. But she could not sit by while Ingrith made bold and erroneous statements about *her* kingdom. "May I ask what you are implying, Majesty?" she said, keeping her voice even.

"Innocent men are being slaughtered on the Moors," Ingrith answered, "and *she's* talking about faeries!"

At that moment, Arabella, who had spent much of the dinner under the table fussing at Diaval's leg, took the opportunity to lunge up and attack. Diaval shouted as he tried to move out of the way. Just before the cat's long claws reached Diaval's face, Maleficent flicked a stream of green magic, lifting the cat into the air above the table, where she hovered like a feline chandelier.

"*Contain* your animal," Maleficent said, her voice icy, "or I will."

"Why, if I didn't know better," Ingrith said, taking in the scene, "I would say you were making a threat."

"So do you?" Maleficent asked.

Queen Ingrith raised an eyebrow. "Do I what?"

"Know better?"

King John slammed a hand on the table. "That's enough!" he shouted, finally sounding like the king he was. "We're here to celebrate."

Maleficent let go of her grip on Arabella. The cat fell on the table, then jumped under Ingrith's chair.

Ingrith nodded. "Forgive me," she said. "He's right. We must remember why we're here. I would like to offer a toast: to the start of a new life—for Aurora." She paused, lifting her goblet and her eyes, so they were locked on Maleficent. "You have done an admirable job, Maleficent, going against your own nature to raise this child. But now Aurora will finally get the love of a real family. A real mother." She paused, and the air seemed to grow heavier. Aurora shifted on her seat. She felt uncomfortable, as though she were hearing a conversation she shouldn't. "Because that's the one thing I regret," Ingrith finished. "Never having a daughter of my own. But tonight that changes. Tonight I consider Aurora . . . my own."

CHAPTER SEVEN

MALEFICENT STARED AT THE PALE WISP OF A WOMAN IN FRONT OF HER. HOW DARE SHE? HOW DARE SHE SIT THERE IN HER GAUDY GOWN AND HURL ACCUSATIONS HIDDEN BEHIND FALSE COMPLIMENTS? Did Ingrith really have no idea what Maleficent was capable of, what magic she controlled? Did she think that she could throw a single dinner and take Aurora away—just like that? Did she truly think she was going to be Aurora's mother?

No. Ingrith was a fool. And that was all she would ever be.

But unfortunately, she was a fool who would not stop talking. And with every word Ingrith spoke, Maleficent's patience lessened and her anger grew.

Slowly, the Dark Fey rose to her feet. As she took her staff in her hand, it began to glow, illuminating her face—and everything around her—in an eerie shade of green. Wind blew through the room even though not a single window was open. Candles flickered and were snuffed out as the scarf on Maleficent's head whipped away, revealing her large black horns.

She heard Aurora's voice pleading with her to stop, but she couldn't. She had tried to play the game nicely. She had agreed to this ridiculous charade out of love for Aurora. But she was not going to sit there while Ingrith threatened to take away the only family she would ever have. Aurora was hers. She would never be part of Ingrith's family—not if Maleficent could help it.

Pushing back her seat, Ingrith brought a hand to her chest as more green magic swirled. "We've opened our home to a witch!" she said. Then she nodded to Percival and Gerda. "We must protect the king!"

As Percival left to get help, Gerda slipped from the room. Maleficent paid neither of them any mind. Her eyes remained focused on the king and queen. All kindness had vanished from King John's face. In that moment, Maleficent could see how the king had

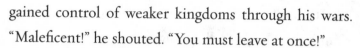

gained control of weaker kingdoms through his wars. "Maleficent!" he shouted. "You must leave at once!"

In response, Maleficent spread her wings. She would never take orders from *any* king—ever. Behind her, the doors flew open and a dozen royal guards burst in, led by Percival. One beat of her wings sent them flying back. Fleeing through the open door, Diaval disappeared. Maleficent could only hope he would find his way to safety. She didn't have time to do more.

Rising to his feet, King John put a reassuring hand on Ingrith's arm as she cowered into him. The green smoke thickened and began to swirl around Maleficent's feet as her rage continued to build. Ingrith could cower and shake all she wanted. It would do her no good. "There shall be *no* wedding!" Maleficent thundered.

Ingrith let out a weak cry and collapsed against her husband. "John," she said, her voice trembling, "I'm so frightened."

The king, holding up his wife, winced slightly and then once more looked at Maleficent. "I said get out." But as he spoke, his face paled and his grip loosened on

Ingrith. "What has she done?" he murmured. Then he slumped to the ground, falling unconscious in front of the golden cradle that had begun it all.

Dropping to her knees, Ingrith tried to wake the king. But he wouldn't stir. As Phillip rushed over, Ingrith turned and pointed at Maleficent. "A curse!" she shrieked. "Maleficent has cursed the king!"

Maleficent took an involuntary step back. The king had fallen on his own. She had been across the room. "I did no such—" she started in protest.

But Ingrith cut her off. "A *curse!*" she screamed again, the word echoing in the now silent room.

Maleficent stared at the scene in front of her. Phillip was trying, in vain, to wake his father while Ingrith stared at her with cold, accusing eyes. Images from long before, when she had been wrongfully accused, flashed through her mind. She began to shake her head. No. This was not happening. This could not be happening again. Slowly, she turned, looking for support from Aurora. But she saw that Aurora was frozen.

Aurora's eyes were locked on the fallen king. Then

she slowly lifted her head, turning until her eyes met Maleficent's.

"This was not my doing," Maleficent said, unsure why she had to say the words aloud. Aurora should know she wouldn't do such a thing.

"He simply asked you to leave!" Aurora said, her voice full of anguish. "Wake him up! Wake him up right now!"

"Aurora," Maleficent said, reaching out her hand. They didn't belong here. She had said so all along. They could cover up her horns and play nice, but it was a foolish and pointless game—and now someone had lost. It was time to go. Aurora would come with her and leave this horrible place. That was what would happen. She stretched her hand out again.

Aurora backed away.

The movement was as painful to Maleficent as if Aurora had reached out and slapped her. Maleficent felt something sharp in her chest, and it took her a moment to realize that it was the breaking of her own heart. Aurora—the girl she knew better than anyone, the human who had given her hope—was now an alien species to her. The pain sharpened as Aurora joined Phillip and his mother. As all three hovered around the fallen King John, they looked every inch the portrait of a family.

The sound of footsteps pulled Maleficent out of her pain. Looking around, she saw the guards were beginning to raise their weapons. Maleficent had no choice. If she stayed, the guards would take her prisoner—or worse.

With one last look at Aurora, Maleficent spread her wings and then, lifting into the air, swooped toward a high window. Crashing through it, she burst into the night sky.

As shattered glass rained down, Maleficent flapped her wings and headed toward the Moors. But then something suddenly zipped past her. Over her shoulder, she saw Gerda standing at the top of the castle. In the engineer's arms was a huge crossbow. As Maleficent watched, Gerda pulled back her arm and let another arrow fly. Maleficent ducked out of the way. Turning, she lifted her hands, ready to send her magic back at Gerda. But to her surprise, the engineer didn't seem worried. She placed a small round object into the bow. Once more, the woman took aim and fired. Only now, instead of an arrow, a bullet zipped through the air.

It moved so fast Maleficent didn't have time to dodge it. A moment later, she cried out as the bullet struck her stomach. Her flesh hissed and smoked as iron met it. Trying to get away, Maleficent pumped her wings. But the pain was too much. She hovered in the air for another moment before plunging down, down, down into the cold and murky depths of the river. Maleficent fought against the current. Each swing of her arms was excruciating. She had no choice but to let the water take her. With no resistance, the current pulled her quickly toward the large waterfall that marked the end of the river. The falls pounded over a rocky cliff, dumping water—and soon Maleficent—into the ocean below.

The last thing she saw before the pain overcame

her was Gerda staring down at her from atop the castle, triumph in her eyes. As far as she was concerned, the mighty Maleficent was no more.

Inside the castle, the king was rushed to his chambers. Aurora and Phillip watched as guards gently placed the unresponsive man on his bed, then they kneeled beside him. The queen remained standing, her hands clasped in front of her, as the royal doctor began his examination.

"This magic—we have no tools to reverse it," he said as he worked. "There must be a lesion—proof of her witchery!" He started to lift the king's sleeve.

"Please," Ingrith said, finally moving, "leave His Majesty his dignity. We all saw what she did to him." She lifted a hand to her mouth, as if the thought alone was too much for her to handle. In truth, she needed to keep anyone from seeing the satisfied smile on her face. So many things had gone wrong over the course of the dinner, but some had gone deliciously right.

Aurora pushed herself to her feet and approached Ingrith. The queen willed herself not to recoil as the girl

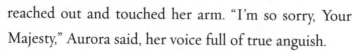

reached out and touched her arm. "I'm so sorry, Your Majesty," Aurora said, her voice full of true anguish.

"A curse upon our king is a curse upon our kingdom. All he wanted was peace," Ingrith said.

Her words made Aurora's guilt grow tenfold. "This is my fault—" she started.

But the queen cut her off. She needed Aurora to see her as a kind, trustworthy figure. She needed to make sure the girl would love her, not Maleficent. "You have nothing to apologize for, my dear," she said. "A beautiful rose is not responsible for her thorns."

Then Ingrith approached the king's bedside. Out of the corner of her eye, she saw Phillip take Aurora's hand to comfort her. "Maleficent is a threat to everyone," Ingrith went on. She looked back at Aurora. "Especially you. We'll do our best to protect you." She smiled as Aurora seemed to shrink within herself. Good. She wanted Aurora to be scared. Worried. That would make her job easier.

"There must be a way to reverse this," Phillip said.

Ingrith felt a momentary pang of guilt when she saw

the devastation on his face. But her guilt vanished when he spoke again.

"Mother, have you tried kissing him?" he asked. "True love—"

"I doubt that would work," Ingrith said quickly.

"Please," Phillip begged.

Ingrith stifled a groan. She found her son's—and his father's—ridiculous notions of romance incredibly annoying. "A kiss is just a kiss," she said flatly.

"It could save him," Aurora added.

By now, everyone in the room was looking at Ingrith. She had no choice. If she refused, she would appear heartless, and she needed everyone to believe she cared. "Very well," she said, moving closer to the bed.

The doctor stepped away as she stood over her husband. Leaning down, she tried to keep her disgust at bay as she lifted the man's limp hand to her face. She kissed it quickly before dropping it back to the bed. But when she glanced behind her, she saw that Phillip, Aurora, and the others were all still watching expectantly.

She would have to actually kiss him.

The thought made her stomach wrench. But there was no other way. Once more, she leaned down. Hovering close to his face, she whispered softly, "You pathetic little man. You wanted peace—now rest in peace forever." Then she kissed him on the lips.

Straightening up, she waited a beat. When nothing happened, she willed tears into her eyes and turned back to her son. "I told you," she said. "This is no fairy tale."

At her words, Aurora moved to the door. "I have to return to the Moors," she said. "It's the only way."

"Aurora!" Phillip called, chasing after her. "Wait!"

Aurora's face was awash with emotions as she looked among Phillip, the king, and the queen. "I have to go to her, Phillip," she said.

"It's the middle of the night," Phillip said.

Aurora shook her head. "She will break the curse," she said. "I know she will."

"Then I'm coming with you," the prince proclaimed boldly.

"I need to see her alone," Aurora said gently. "And you should stay with your family." She smiled up at

Phillip, tears in her eyes. Inside, Ingrith's stomach lurched at the unspoken emotion between the two. She really would have to do something about Phillip and his weak heart.

Phillip frowned. "You *are* my family," he said, not giving up.

Ingrith had had enough. Things would be easier without Aurora around. "Let her go, Phillip," she said. "Maybe she can save him."

Aurora gave the queen a grateful look. "Please," she said, turning to one of the guards, "I'll need a horse."

Aurora followed a guard out of the room, and Ingrith was pleased to see her go. Yes, things were indeed shaping up nicely. Now that Aurora was off to the Moors, Ingrith could continue with her work.

CHAPTER EIGHT

THE MOORS HAD NEVER SEEMED SO FAR AWAY.

AS THE WHITE HORSE BENEATH HER FINALLY PLUNGED THROUGH THE DARK AND QUIET MOORS, AURORA DESPERATELY CALLED OUT TO MALEFICENT. But she was met with no response. By the time she reached her castle and galloped over the bridge made of trees and leaves, tears were streaming down her cheeks. A full moon bathed the green castle in bright white light. At any other time, she would have marveled at the beauty, but now all she could see was the emptiness.

How could it all have gone so terribly wrong? She had not expected the dinner to be perfect. That would have been lunacy on her part. But she could never have predicted the debacle that had unfolded. Or its outcome.

"Maleficent!" Aurora screamed, jumping from her

horse and racing inside. "Maleficent!" The only answer was her echo. No one was there.

A wave of panic overtook her as she walked back out onto the bridge. Her eyes scanned the surrounding moors before turning to the high crag that dominated the far border. It was Maleficent's favorite spot. Perhaps she had gone there. "Godmother! Please," Aurora cried; the pain was so deep. "Just come back."

No matter how many times she called, Maleficent did not appear. Finally, exhausted—both mentally and physically—Aurora sat on the steps to the castle. She let the tears fall as Pinto appeared and curled up beside her. Taking some small comfort from the little hedgehog faerie, Aurora absently ran her fingers along the creature's back. Hearing footsteps, she turned hopefully. But it was only Diaval.

"She's not in the Moors," he said as he approached. "No one has seen her." He looked as miserable as Aurora felt.

She stood, ran to him, and threw her arms around him. In the midst of the terrible dinner, she hadn't noticed him disappear. Now she was glad he had. She needed a friend. "Diaval," she said, squeezing him tightly. "I'm so happy to see you."

Diaval returned the hug, his thin arms trembling. Maleficent was as important to him as she was to Aurora. "She's nowhere to be found," he said, pulling away after a moment. "What if she never comes back?"

"I have to find her," Aurora said. *I have to because this is all my fault,* she added silently.

"You?" Diaval said. "What about me? I could be stuck as a human forever! Look at me—I'm hideous!"

His attempt at lightening the mood worked for a moment. Aurora smiled briefly. But then she shook her head. "She needs to break the curse! It's the only way."

Diaval frowned. "Have you considered the possibility—"

"What?" Aurora interrupted, confused.

"That it wasn't her curse," Diaval said softly.

Aurora shook her head. She had been there. She had seen her godmother's green magic and watched the fury in her eyes. She knew how much Maleficent hated humans and how angry she had been. "Who else could do such a thing?" she finally asked. *No,* she thought when Diaval didn't reply. He was wrong. Maleficent *had* cursed the king.

But that meant she could fix it. She could fix it all, if only Aurora knew where she had gone.

Maleficent was lying on something soft. She could feel it pressing against her skin, keeping her warm and comfortable. She dared not open her eyes. Not yet. She feared that if she did, she might discover the warmth was a dream.

She had only vague memories of the moments after she had been shot. She remembered falling for what felt like forever and the sensation of the water as she crashed into it. She remembered seeing the engineer on the tower and then her eyes closing as the weight of the water and her wound became too much and she was pulled along with the current until she went over a massive waterfall. Once again she had fallen, only to land in the colder water of the ocean beyond Ulstead. Caught in the current, she had begun to drift.

And then someone, or something, had pulled her from the water. She remembered being lifted into the sky and the sound of wings beating close to her ears. She could have sworn there was a shimmering blue light and then wind on her cheeks. Her eyes had flickered open a while later, and she had only the briefest glimmers of huge towering rocks and crashing waves before whoever was carrying her headed down and into what looked like a cave. Then her eyes had closed again as she gave in to the overwhelming pain.

Now she lay still, trying to make sense of what had happened. Finally, she opened her eyes. The comfortable bed she was lying on was made of moss. A high curved ceiling, made of tightly woven grasses, rose above her, giving the room a natural warmth. Hearing a whoosh behind her, Maleficent tried to sit up.

But when she did, pain shot through her. Lying back down, she gingerly placed a hand on her wound. The

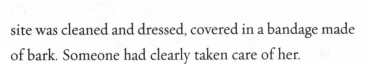

site was cleaned and dressed, covered in a bandage made of bark. Someone had clearly taken care of her.

But who?

Hearing voices outside the room, Maleficent shifted nervously. Wrapping her wings tightly around her, she forced herself to a sitting position. The voices were growing louder, more heated. For the first time in a long while, Maleficent was frightened.

She cautiously lowered her feet to the floor. The pain was terrible, but she wanted to be standing when the owners of the voices revealed themselves. Walking slowly across the floor, she made her way toward a circular opening in the wall. Peering through, she found herself looking into a dark, empty tunnel.

Taking a deep breath, Maleficent entered the tunnel. She could see a small shaft of light at the other end and limped toward it. As the light grew brighter, the tunnel widened, finally opening into a huge cavernous circle. Maleficent's eyes widened as she took in the room that went up, up, up, its sides covered with branches. It was as if she were inside a giant bird's nest.

Her eyes became wider still when she saw, standing in the middle of the nest, ten towering figures. Each figure had a large set of horns on its head and dark heavy wings hanging from its back.

Dark Fey.

Maleficent gasped. They looked just like her. But how could that be? She'd thought she was the only one of her kind. As she got closer, she saw that one of the Dark Fey was holding up the iron bullet that had pierced her stomach. His skin was dry and cracked, like a desert riverbed, and his eyes were angry as the bullet sizzled between his fingers.

"Do you hear it?" the Dark Fey, named Borra, said as the bullet continued to sizzle. He lifted it to his ear. "It's a message from the humans. I hear it loud and clear. Time for us to die."

Another one of the Dark Fey stepped forward. Maleficent watched as he shook his head. His skin was darker and smoother than Borra's. He was more muscular, and his stance was that of a warrior. Where Borra's eyes were full of anger, this fey's eyes held sadness and an ageless wisdom. He studied the bullet closely. "Humans have been using iron against us for centuries," he pointed out.

There were murmurs of agreement from a few of the other fey. "And we are almost extinct because of it, Conall!" Borra shouted angrily at the warrior. "They pulled iron from the earth. Made their shields and swords and drove us underground!" He once again lifted the bullet for all to see. "But *this* will finish us. I call for war right now!"

Maleficent stepped back into the shadows. She had clearly stumbled upon a war council of some kind. Borra's words echoed in her mind. *Almost extinct,* he had said. That was why she had spent her life believing she was alone. But she wasn't. And these fey, at least some of them, were as distrusting of humans as she was. As the room filled with voices echoing Borra's call to war, she noticed that Conall was quiet. He waited for everyone to settle before he spoke again.

"There are too many humans," he finally said when he had the group's attention. "Too many kingdoms."

"So you would wait for them to find us?" Borra retorted. "To kill us all!"

"We can't win," Conall said. "Not this way."

Borra shook his head. "You're wrong, Conall," he said. "We have something they didn't plan on." Then, to Maleficent's surprise, Borra lifted into the air and flew—straight at her. As he hovered in front of her, his eyes locked on hers. She took another step back. How long had he known she was standing there? "We have . . . *her*," Borra went on. "She has powers none of us possess."

"She is wounded, Borra," Conall pointed out.

That was it. Maleficent stepped into the light. She did not need these strangers talking about her as though she were a pawn in some game she didn't even know about. "Who are you?" she yelled, making her voice as loud as possible despite the pain it caused her.

In a flash, Borra flew closer to her, putting his face mere inches from her own. He breathed in deeply, his eyes glowing. "You reek of human," he said with a sneer. "Maybe I'm wrong about you. Maybe Conall should have left you for dead at the bottom of the sea."

Maleficent's eyes shifted to the handsome warrior fey. So it had been Conall who had carried her across the sea and to this place. She couldn't help wondering . . . why?

Shaking his head, Borra pulled back. "No," he went on, his tone threatening. "It's in there, isn't it? It's inside you." Once again, he moved closer, his eyes dark and menacing.

Reflexively, Maleficent raised her hand. A thin stream of green magic pooled at her fingertips, and then, with a flick of her hand, she sent it right at Borra. It hit him square in the chest, slamming him into the far wall. Maleficent, drained from the small use of her magic, dropped to the ground, panting.

Borra smiled wickedly where he lay. Maleficent had done just what he had hoped: given a demonstration. She had shown everyone there how powerful she was, even in her current state. "You see?" he said proudly. "There is evil in her heart. And that is what will save us all."

"She needs to heal," Conall said, his calm voice oddly comforting to Maleficent.

Borra nodded. "You will help her, Conall," he said. "And when she is ready, we go to war."

His message delivered, Borra flew off. The others waited a moment before they, too, disappeared into the depths of the Nest.

Only Conall remained. He made his way to Maleficent, then stopped in front of her. He reached out a hand to help her up, but she pushed him away. His eyes lingered on her wound, which, due to her exertion, had reopened and was oozing thick black blood.

Self-conscious, Maleficent touched her bandaged wound. Perhaps she had been quick—and wrong—to push him away so forcefully. "It was you who saved me?" she asked.

Conall nodded. He turned to go and then looked back at her. "Come," he said. "I'll show you who we are." He moved toward a large hole in the floor, which Maleficent hadn't noticed during Borra's blustering. Stepping to the edge, Conall turned his back to the hole. He looked at Maleficent, his kind eyes brightening, and then he fell back and disappeared.

Inching forward, Maleficent peered over the rim of the hole. She couldn't see anything. It was impossible to tell if there was a floor, or rocks, or something worse below. Still, she was curious. Getting to her feet, she moved so that her toes curled around the rim. Taking a deep breath, she lifted her foot . . .

And fell.

Maleficent tumbled through the air. Desperately attempting to gain control of the free fall, she tried to flap her wings. But she was too weak, and they wouldn't move. She just kept falling. And she would have continued if Conall hadn't caught her.

"Don't—" Maleficent started.

"Easy," Conall replied.

The protest faded on her lips as she looked around. They were in some sort of makeshift hideout. It was dark, and a fine layer of mist covered everything. But through it, Maleficent could see dozens of Dark Fey moving through the nest-like space. Some were alone.

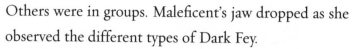

Others were in groups. Maleficent's jaw dropped as she observed the different types of Dark Fey.

As they moved through the Nest, Conall explained. Tundra fey were pale, their wings and hair white. Smaller than the other fey, they were close to the ground, both physically and emotionally. Then there were the colorful jungle fey, with long limbs for jumping and swinging. Their wings were bright, each pair unique and compact. As Maleficent watched, one jungle fey spread her wings and then pulled them tight to her body so they virtually disappeared. *That would have been helpful at dinner,* Maleficent thought wryly.

And there were more. The desert fey—like Borra— had gold-flecked skin and substantial jointed wings. And the forest fey were Maleficent's kind. It was obvious from their massive dark wings and proportions similar to hers.

But Conall revealed that no matter the kind, they were all Dark Fey. "Same as you," he said.

Maleficent was quiet as she watched the dozens of

fey flit into and out of the Nest, ignoring her presence, because to them she was not unique. "How many are there?" she finally asked. "Of . . . us?"

"We are all that remain," Conall said, landing on another level of the Nest far below the one they had come from.

"My entire life—" Maleficent began, but her emotions overcame her. She had to turn away. Composing herself, she was silent for a long while, taking it all in. Conall had been somber when he said this was all that was left of the fey. But to her, the number seemed huge.

Conall motioned to a ledge farther below them. Five young fey were standing back, nervously eyeing the edge. Their wings were spread out behind them as Udo, an older Tundra fey, instructed them. Maleficent recognized him from earlier. She watched as Udo began to nudge the group forward until they were inches from the edge. Maleficent saw the fear in the young feys' eyes, and then, with a mighty push, Udo sent them all off, into the air. Maleficent gasped as they began to fall.

"Those young ones should be connected to nature,"

Conall said, his eyes glued to the fey. "Instead, they're banished like the rest of us. Raised in exile."

"They belong on the Moors," Maleficent said, nodding in agreement. "In the snow, in the deserts . . ."

Conall sighed. "As more human kingdoms emerged, we kept moving," he explained, "hiding in all the corners of the earth. But we knew they would find us eventually—even when we returned to our true home."

Maleficent watched him as he spoke. His face was full of unspoken pain, and she wondered how much he had seen and sacrificed. Her eyes drifted from the warrior to the young fey, who were now swooping and laughing as they caught the wind and flew around the Nest. Their faces were full of joy and innocence. They should never have to see what Conall—or Maleficent—had seen.

"I can protect them," she said.

"How?" Conall asked. His tone was kind, but there was defensiveness to it. "By waging war against the humans? Even the one you raised as your own?" He paused, gauging Maleficent's reaction. When she didn't

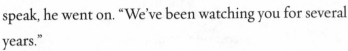

speak, he went on. "We've been watching you for several years."

At this, Maleficent startled. "And yet you stay hidden?" she asked, confused—and suddenly angry. If she had known there were others like her . . . what might her life have been like?

"Because you were doing something we never thought possible," Conall explained. "You were showing us the way forward."

Curious about what he meant, Maleficent narrowed her eyes and waited to hear more. She had simply been trying to survive and raise Aurora to love the Moors as she did.

Conall continued. "Maybe we don't have to hide from humans," he told her. "Maybe we can exist without fear and war. Maybe we can find a way . . . together."

Maleficent's response was swift. "That will never happen." The pain in her stomach was a reminder of what happened when humans and faeries tried to coexist. The memory of Aurora looking at her with distrust was another.

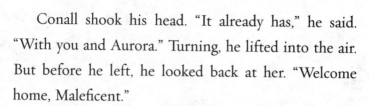

Conall shook his head. "It already has," he said. "With you and Aurora." Turning, he lifted into the air. But before he left, he looked back at her. "Welcome home, Maleficent."

Maleficent's thoughts whirled around her head. *Home.* Was that where she was now? Could she learn to trust the Nest—and the other fey? She had spent so long feeling out of place, even among the Moors. Was this where she belonged?

Summoning all her strength, she slowly flew back toward the top of the Nest. If that was true, she wondered why she still felt unhappy.

CHAPTER NINE

AURORA HAD GIVEN UP. AFTER HOURS OF SEARCHING THE MOORS, SHE REALIZED THAT MALEFICENT WASN'T COMING HOME. AT LEAST, NOT RIGHT AWAY. With a heavy heart, she got back on her horse and rode to Castle Ulstead. The huge structure was dark when she arrived, with only a few candles lit to guide her way down the hallway to her room.

Her room. It seemed strange to think of it that way. Her real room was back in her own castle, but Phillip had insisted that she stay close while they tried to figure out what to do for the king. Aurora had had no choice but to say yes.

Now, stepping forward, she sighed. She was exhausted. All she wanted to do was lie down, close her eyes, and have a few moments of dreamless sleep. But it seemed her wish was not to be granted.

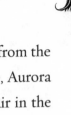

"We've been worried." Ingrith's voice came from the darkness and startled Aurora. Lighting a candle, Aurora saw that the queen was sitting in an ornate chair in the corner of the room. Slowly, Ingrith got to her feet and began to move toward Aurora.

"Your Majesty," Aurora said when she had composed herself. "I tried to find her." Just speaking of her failure made fresh tears well in Aurora's eyes.

For a moment, anger flashed on Queen Ingrith's face. But it disappeared as quickly as it had come, and was replaced by a look of sympathy. "My heart breaks for you," Ingrith said, moving closer. "She has brought a cloud of darkness over your happiness. I know she was against this marriage—never trusted your instincts." Ingrith stopped, shaking her head sadly.

Aurora struggled to fight back tears. The truth in Ingrith's words stung. Maleficent had made it clear that she didn't want Aurora to marry Phillip. But Aurora had hoped Maleficent's love for her would overcome the fear.

It had not.

Ingrith went on, her voice growing more intense. "When I saw her at dinner, with her horns covered, bent cowering . . ." She paused and then shrugged ever so slightly. "Well, it's no wonder she lashed out."

Aurora found herself nodding. She could see the anger in Maleficent's eyes. She could hear her caustic tone as she talked of Phillip and his "romantic" gestures. She remembered the disgust on Maleficent's face when Aurora giddily told her Phillip had said he loved her for the first time. Maybe love wasn't something Maleficent could understand.

But then other memories flooded over her: Maleficent waking her with a kiss. Fighting Stefan to protect her. Giving her the Moors so she would have a home full of joy instead of sadness. Aurora shook her head in protest.

She could reminisce about the good moments, but Ingrith was right. Of course Maleficent had lashed out. The whole evening had gone against who she was. And one could fight their true nature for only so long before finally giving in.

"I just don't know what to do," Aurora finally said, her voice shaking.

At her words, the queen seemed to perk up. "You do truly love him, don't you? My son?"

Aurora nodded, biting her lip. "Deeply."

"Then it is love that will heal you. It's what heals us all. Let's move forward together," Ingrith said. "As a family."

Aurora let out a surprised cry. She had not anticipated such a response. Nor was she prepared for it. *Family.* The simple word made her feel less alone and quelled the pain filling her chest. Aurora walked to the queen and threw her arms around her. Ingrith smiled and even began to stroke Aurora's hair.

Aurora was still hugging Ingrith when the door opened.

Phillip's voice echoed through the chamber. "Mother?" he asked, his eyes locked on Aurora. "What's going on?"

Ingrith pulled free from Aurora's embrace as Phillip entered the room. She took Aurora's hand and placed it in his. "I have made a decision," she said. "In the name of your father, the wedding will take place in three days' time." Her statement delivered, she smiled at the couple and then left the room.

In the wake of her departure, Aurora and Phillip stood in shocked silence. "Aurora," Phillip finally said. "We don't have to think about a wedding now."

Aurora shook her head. Ingrith was right. They owed it to everyone—especially the king. They could not let the darkness of Maleficent's actions, or King John's dire circumstances, ruin what was supposed to be a joyous time for their two kingdoms. If they backed away from hardship, it would set the tone for the rest of their reign. But if she and Phillip stayed strong, showing their love was powerful enough to overcome anything, it would make for a wonderful beginning.

"What about Maleficent?" Phillip asked after Aurora explained her choice.

"I believe she's gone," she said. "Forever."

• • •

As the sun rose over Castle Ulstead, news of the wedding spread swiftly. Villagers jumped into action, eager to help make the wedding perfect. Bakers began baking. Florists began gathering. Street sweepers began sweeping. The air was full of happy anticipation.

But far away, deep in the heart of the Nest, Maleficent was unaware of how quickly things were changing. She was not looking to the future; instead, she was trying to make sense of the past. At her request, Conall had brought Maleficent to the Great Tree.

Walking around the base of the enormous ancient tree, Maleficent felt small. It was the most sacred site in the Nest. Conall told her no one knew just how old the tree was, only that it had been there when they came. Elaborate inscrutable etchings were carved into the curved walls that surrounded the base of the tree. Over the years, the room had become a shrine, and the history of their kind was written on its walls.

Conall paused in front of a huge rock. In the center,

preserved in thick orange amber, was a set of bones. "A phoenix," Conall said when he saw the question on Maleficent's face. "It is said that the Dark Fey began with her—evolved over centuries. But soon our time will end. . . ." His voice trailed off, and he turned to look at Maleficent. "Unless you can save us."

Maleficent was confused. A day earlier, he had seen her use the darkness in her to slam Borra against a wall. She had seen Conall's disappointment at the time and known that he wanted her to be better than that. Yet now he was saying she could save them all?

"In your hands you hold life and death," Conall went on cryptically. "Destruction and rebirth. But nature's greatest power is the power of true transformation. You transformed when you lost your wings. When you raised Aurora and when you found love in the middle of pain." Conall moved closer so that he was almost touching Maleficent.

She shifted on her feet. There was something about the strong, handsome fey that made her nervous.

"You are the last of her descendants." His gaze moved

to the phoenix's bones. "Her blood is your own. I'm asking you to take all of your fury, all of your pain—and *not* use it. Peace will be the Dark Fey's final transformation."

Suddenly, the sound of flapping wings echoed through the chamber. Dragging her eyes from Conall, Maleficent watched as Borra landed nearby. As usual, he was frowning, his eyes full of unleashed rage. She couldn't tell if it was directed at her or the world. She guessed it was a bit of both.

Giving Borra only the briefest acknowledgement, Conall continued. Maleficent wasn't sure why he was so determined to get her on his side, but she listened. "The Moors are our last true nature on earth. And yet you named a human as queen. A daughter you cared for—"

"I have no daughter!" Maleficent shrieked.

The words were out of her mouth before Maleficent could stop them. Hearing them out loud made her heart ache, and she reflexively put a hand to the still healing wound on her stomach. Up until that very moment, she had not allowed herself to admit that what she believed was true: Aurora was no longer a part of her life. Now it felt real—and raw.

Seeing the pain on her face, Borra smiled cruelly. "We've just heard there's going to be a wedding at the castle in three days," he said, giving the reason for his arrival. "Humans will come from all over." Borra stalked closer. He looked thrilled by the news, which confused Maleficent until he added, "We will kill the king and queen of Ulstead—and the young prince."

Borra's words echoed off the walls until they faded, leaving nothing but silence. Maleficent stood motionless while her mind reeled. She wanted the king and queen of Ulstead to suffer for what they had done. And Phillip, too. In a flash, she remembered Aurora's feelings. If he were to come to harm, what would that do to Aurora?

A small bitter thought crept into her mind. Aurora would get her heart broken. Would that be so wrong? Should Maleficent even care? Her fingers traced the outline of her wound. A few days earlier, the idea of

Aurora's feeling pain would have filled Maleficent with fury. Now she just felt numb.

Shrugging, she turned to stare at the phoenix. Let Borra plan his war. She would see what rose from the ashes.

CHAPTER TEN

INGRITH WAS GROWING BORED. WHEN SHE HAD ANNOUNCED THE WEDDING, SHE KNEW THERE WOULD BE COUNTLESS DETAILS TO OVERSEE. BUT SHE HAD FAILED TO CONSIDER JUST HOW EXHAUSTING FEIGN-ING HAPPINESS COULD BE—OR HOW MANY HOURS WOULD BE REQUIRED. For the past two days she had pretended to delight over wedding cake options and fawn over floral arrangements. She had listened to countless musicians vie for the chance to play the wed-ding march. She had flattered Phillip and Aurora and applauded with joy when they chose their first song.

She was tired of it.

Now Ingrith stood in Aurora's chambers, waiting for the girl to come out from behind the large dress-ing screen that stood along the far wall. She heard the girl giggling with the handmaidens as she dressed, and then . . . silence. A moment later, Aurora emerged.

If Ingrith had had a warm bone in her body, she would have done something motherly, like gasp or clutch her hands to her heart, as she watched her future daughter-in-law glide closer. The girl *was* breathtaking. Even in the simple cream gown without embellishments, not even a single gem, she glowed. Her cheeks were flushed, and her lips, which she now bit nervously, were a perfect shade of pink. Flowing out from her long hair was a lace veil, the pattern simple and delicate, like a spider's web.

But Ingrith was cold. So she said simply and without feeling, "You look stunning, Aurora."

Aurora smiled happily, not picking up on the flat tone of Ingrith's voice. "I'm so glad you like it, Your Majesty," she said.

As Ingrith moved closer, she gasped and brought a hand to her throat. She immediately stopped walking. "Oh, my," she struggled to say. "I can hardly breathe."

"Is something wrong?" Aurora asked, concern spreading across her face.

Ingrith bowed her head, giving her enough time to compose her features. Then she looked up with a frown on her face. "My allergies," she said by way of explanation. "I can detect the slightest bit of dirt and dust—and that dress comes straight from the Moors, does it not?" She eyed the gown as though it were alive.

"Yes," Aurora said, touching the lace gingerly with the tip of her finger. "I'm so sorry. What can I do?"

"Perhaps," Ingrith said as though she had a sudden and wholly new idea, "you could try this on?" She motioned to two servants, who had been waiting for her signal. Quickly, they ushered over a wedding gown that required both of them to carry it.

The dress was everything Aurora's was not. While hers was plain, allowing the simplicity of the design to make it beautiful, this gown was elaborate. Every inch was studded with jewels, and the lace was complex; the lines created a pattern that seemed hard and rigid, whereas the lace on Aurora's was gentle and soft. And while Aurora's train had been pieced together from material found in the Moors, the train on this dress was nearly ten feet long. Everything about it was heavy; it was more like armor than a wedding gown.

"I wore it when I married the king," Ingrith said, eyeing the dress proudly. She turned and saw Aurora composing her face as she, too, looked upon the gown.

"I'm sure it's perfect," Aurora said after a moment. Her voice was tender and the words were polite, but Aurora would wear the gown only because she was too nice to say no.

"So am I," Ingrith replied. She instructed the handmaidens on where to put Aurora's dress from the Moors. Then she said her good-byes. The queen was done with this nonsense for now. She had other, more important matters to attend to.

Ingrith stepped out of the room and made her way down the hall to her chambers. She glanced around to make sure no one was watching and then slipped inside. While it was not unusual for her to be entering her own chambers, Ingrith preferred the sense of security that came with a stealth entrance. Moments later she was descending toward the laboratory.

As she entered, she saw Lickspittle standing in front of a beaker filled with charcoal-colored sand. He held a small pair of tweezers, which contained a single flake of glowing gold powder. Her eyes narrowed as she took in the pixie's protective clothing. *Is that really necessary?* she wondered. Lickspittle *was* fond of the theatrical, but the homemade gas mask seemed a bit much.

Sighing, she moved closer. At the same time, Lickspittle painstakingly added the flake of powder to the sand. There was a puff—and the sand turned from dark gray to shimmering red. In the surrounding jars, faeries were making faces at Lickspittle, unconcerned by the experiment happening in front of them.

Then Ingrith stepped out of the shadows.

As fear flashed across the faeries' faces, Lickspittle held up a hand. "Don't distract me!" he yelled at them.

"Lickspittle . . ."

Hearing the queen's voice, Lickspittle paled behind

his gas mask. As he ripped it off his head, his eyes filled with fright. "Eep!" he squeaked. "Forgive me, Your Majesty," he said, backpedaling as fast as his little pixie feet allowed.

Lucky for Lickspittle, Ingrith didn't have the time to punish him for insubordination. "Gerda says you've got something," she said instead. "Does it work?"

Lickspittle's large eyes grew a little larger, and his Adam's apple bobbed up and down as he gulped anxiously. He had told Gerda about the experiment in confidence. It was still in the trial stages. Saying he had something that "worked" was a bit of a stretch. But he couldn't just come out and say no. Not to Ingrith.

"I only had a handful of faerie specimens to work with, and the extraction process is painstaking," he said.

Ingrith pointed to the glowing flower. It had been carefully placed in a thin glass vase. "Extraction from what?" she asked. She was getting annoyed. She had come down expecting something concrete, yet Lickspittle was clearly stalling.

Lickspittle took a skittish step closer to her. "Tomb Bloom flowers," he explained. "They grow from a faerie's grave and contain their very essence." He gingerly touched a petal, his face turning solemn for a moment before his eyes flashed with renewed energy. "The ratio of flower extract to iron powder has to be just right—"

"Show me!" Ingrith said. She didn't want to hear long explanations; she wanted to see results. And honestly, her interest was piqued.

Quickly, Lickspittle turned to the jars. Inside, faeries pushed against the glass. But they had nowhere to go. "Now who will try my faerie dust?" he asked gleefully. He spotted the mushroom faerie, then opened the jar and reached in. But just as he started to pick the specimen up, the mushroom faerie bit down—hard. "Ow!" Lickspittle screeched. Dropping the faerie, Lickspittle turned to another jar. Inside was a meek-looking dandelion faerie. His pale hair floated around him as Lickspittle grabbed him and placed him on the table nearby.

Ingrith leaned forward in anticipation. Lickspittle

took a pinch of the fine red dust he had just created and sprinkled it over the dandelion faerie. As the dust settled onto the creature's skin, the faerie's eyes widened and his mouth opened. A moment later, he became still and transformed into a silent dandelion. The faerie, it seemed, was gone.

A smile spread across Ingrith's face. "No more faeries," she said, picking up the dandelion. She lifted it to her lips and blew. The seeds drifted across the room.

"Your Majesty," Lickspittle said, relieved when he saw the pleasure on the queen's face, "I have plenty of iron powder for my formula, but I'll need Tomb Blooms from the Moors. Lots of them."

Ingrith nodded, her eyes still fixed on the dandelion stalk in her hand. "You'll have all that you need."

She didn't care what it took. Lickspittle would have his supplies. Because now, after all these years of planning, she finally had it: the key to destroying all faerie kind.

And soon she would be able to use it.

CHAPTER ELEVEN

MALEFICENT FELT TERRIBLE.

DAYS HAD PASSED AND HER WOUND CONTINUED TO FESTER. SHE HAD THOUGHT THAT BEING SURROUNDED BY OTHERS OF HER KIND WOULD HELP, THAT THEY MIGHT KNOW A WAY TO TREAT HER INFECTION. But the iron was too powerful. Too human.

Standing in the infirmary, she tried to be patient as one of the healing fey pressed and prodded at her wound. Pain radiated through her body to the tips of her fingers. Reflexively, she bared her fangs. The fey treating her was unbothered.

"How are you feeling?"

At Conall's voice, Maleficent turned. Slowly, she lifted her wings, stretching them so that they nearly touched the far walls. "Strong enough to fight," she answered, forcing her voice to sound firm even though that simple effort had been enough to nearly send her to her knees. She didn't want Conall to think her weak.

The past few days had been spent discussing and planning for the wedding—though not in the way she had imagined when Aurora first told her about the engagement. Then Maleficent had actually hoped to spend *no* time discussing it. She had hoped simply to tell Aurora no and be over with the whole mess. But Aurora had said yes to that ridiculous proposal. And now Maleficent wasn't speaking to Aurora *at all*, let alone about a wedding.

With Borra, the talks were not about whether the marriage should happen; instead, they spoke of battle strategy. And with Conall, it was always about hope and the possibility of reconciliation. But it didn't matter whom Maleficent spoke to or listened to. Seeing the young fey—stuck inside the Nest due to fear of the humans outside—watching them learn to fly . . . it had been a turning point. She was going to fight, no matter the cost.

Conall was silent for a moment after Maleficent's

declaration. She felt his eyes heavy on her. Finally, he nodded. "But when you get inside the castle?" he asked. "When you see her? Will you be strong enough then?"

As he spoke, he moved closer. Maleficent reached out and grabbed his arm, about to tell him to leave her alone. But she hesitated when she felt the ridged flesh beneath her fingers. She looked down. Conall's arms were riddled with burn marks. "Were you a warrior?" she asked. She had assumed he was, despite his opposition to Borra's warlike attitude.

He nodded, his eyes darkening. "For a long time," he answered. "But no more."

"What changed?" Maleficent asked.

"You," he answered.

This surprised Maleficent, and she cocked her head in confusion. He smiled slightly before going on. "And Aurora. You showed me a different way."

Maleficent dropped his arm. That again. Conall's fascination with her relationship with Aurora was getting old. That was in the past. "I told you that was a mistake."

He shook his head. "It wasn't a mistake," he said. "It was a choice. *Your* choice."

She exhaled deeply. Conall was infuriating. Time and again, he told Maleficent that she should not fight. When Borra had said *destroy*, Conall had said *forgive*. He made it clear that she should stay out of the fight and repair her relationship with Aurora. Still, he insisted Maleficent get better. Raising an arm, she gestured around the infirmary and then pointed at her wound. "Why do you want me strong if you don't want me to fight?" she asked.

Conall didn't answer right away. The room became quiet as he gazed at Maleficent. Finally, he gave her the smallest of smiles. "Maybe I'm preparing you for a bigger fight," he answered. Then he left the room.

Maleficent watched him go, her mind racing. Just when she had begun to believe there was nothing left to feel, she had an annoying itch growing in her heart. And it was all Conall's fault.

• • •

Aurora felt ridiculous. She had been dancing—or rather, attempting to dance—for hours around Castle Ulstead's ballroom while Ingrith looked on and Gerda, the queen's aid, played a wedding waltz. Her feet felt like rocks, and her stomach was roaring. She just wanted to sit down and have a snack.

But every time she and Phillip slowed their steps, or Aurora tripped, Ingrith would clap her hands and call, "Again." Aurora felt as though the torture would never end. She had a brief flicker of hope when she made it through an entire waltz without a mistake. But the hope vanished when she saw Ingrith hold up a pair of high heels. "Again," Ingrith called out. So again Aurora and Phillip started to sway—only this time, Aurora wore the most painful footwear she had ever encountered.

Finally, though, it seemed Ingrith was satisfied. Nodding to Gerda, the queen allowed the music to stop. Aurora's shoulders sagged and she looked longingly at one of the chairs. But before she could sit, Ingrith was whisking her back to her dressing chamber to be primped and pampered for afternoon tea.

As Aurora followed her, she tried to stay positive. She had known that agreeing to a wedding in three days would mean things would be rather rushed. But she had never imagined how busy she would be—nor how much she would miss Maleficent and the Moors. Every minute of the past two days had been filled with fittings and teas and consultations and dance lessons. The only time she had seen Phillip was when they were practicing their waltz, and even then Ingrith had always been present. The couple hadn't been able to talk, and she desperately needed a confidant. Despite her knowing Maleficent was gone, there was still a piece of Aurora that hoped she was wrong—and that her godmother would appear and fix everything, sending it all back to normal.

But she was no longer a child. She knew most dreams did not come true.

Now Aurora found herself sitting with the queen and a collection of noblewomen. Ingrith had told her they were the ladies to impress. If they gave their stamp of approval, all of Ulstead would follow. Shifting on her chair, Aurora kept a smile plastered on her face as the women around her spoke. Her hair was done up in an elaborate coif that mirrored Ingrith's, and the dress she wore was conservative, tight, and gray, a hand-me-down from the queen herself. *If Maleficent did come back,* Aurora thought, *she probably wouldn't even recognize me.*

Noticing that one of the noblewomen needed more tea, Aurora smoothly stood and filled the cup. Everyone watched, as if hoping she might spill. But when the tea was poured neatly, they all nodded.

"Your Majesty," one of them said, "she's absolutely lovely."

"And to think of how she was raised," another said, as though Aurora were not right next to her. "By the same evil witch who cursed her."

Aurora felt her face flush. How dare they? They had no idea what her childhood was like. She had enjoyed a wonderful childhood because of, not in spite of, Maleficent. Taking a deep breath, she held up a tray of sweets, hoping to change the subject. "Tarts?" she asked, making her voice as sickly sweet as the desserts themselves.

As the women continued to chat, absently taking the treats from Aurora as though she were invisible, Aurora sighed. When she was sure that no one was paying her any mind, she slipped away.

Racing down the long, soulless hallways, she kept the tears back until she finally reached her room. She pushed open the doors, tore off her uncomfortable shoes, and rushed onto the balcony. She needed air. And silence.

But a moment later, the door opened. Fearing it was Ingrith coming to take her back, she turned. To her relief, it was Phillip. Spotting her on the balcony, he moved to join her.

"Aurora," he said as he took in her watery eyes and sad face, "tell me, what's troubling you?"

She didn't answer immediately. She wasn't sure if she could tell him the truth. But then she found her courage. After all, she was going to marry him—in a day. If she couldn't talk to him now, what was the point?

"I'm not sure I belong here," she finally said, her voice barely a whisper.

Phillip shook his head. "You belong with me," he said.

She smiled. She knew he was trying to reassure her, but his words didn't help. "Everyone's been so kind," she said, taking his hand to show him he was a part of that. "But I've only been here two days and I feel like another person." She stopped and looked deep into Phillip's eyes.

"I know, it's hard. . . ."

She shook her head, the reaction surprising both of them. "No, it's too easy. This jewelry, my hair." She lifted a hand to her perfectly coifed head. "Even my smile has changed. I don't feel like queen of the Moors anymore." As she finished, a prickle of doubt formed in her heart. Had she been wrong to tell Phillip how she felt? But then he squeezed her hand, his warm, open face full of the kindness and light she had fallen in love with in the first place. The prickle began to fade.

"I want to marry the girl I met in the forest. And only her," Phillip said softly. He reached out and brushed

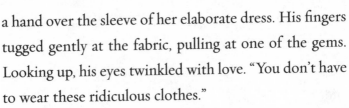

a hand over the sleeve of her elaborate dress. His fingers tugged gently at the fabric, pulling at one of the gems. Looking up, his eyes twinkled with love. "You don't have to wear these ridiculous clothes."

The last of the prickle faded completely away as she moved into Phillip's arms and squeezed him tightly. Of course he would understand. Of course he would know that she was stronger than the foolish women downstairs. He knew her and loved her for all she was; he always had.

But as she turned to watch Phillip leave, she caught sight of her reflection in the mirror. The woman staring back at her was a stranger. An image of Maleficent, her horns covered in fabric, flashed through her mind. Who had she been to ask the Dark Fey to hide who she was? To play dress-up to make others happy?

No wonder Maleficent had gone and never returned. It was terrible to try and be someone you weren't.

The Moors were quiet. Thick clouds had covered the sky and sent the creatures scurrying off to their beds. But

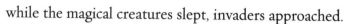

while the magical creatures slept, invaders approached.

Holding up his hand, Percival signaled to the forty or so soldiers waiting behind him. At Queen Ingrith's orders, he had found the young man who had brought the Tomb Bloom to Lickspittle in the first place. Ben had been quick to offer his assistance—as soon as he saw the nice bag of gold Gerda held up. With the boy showing them the way, Percival had led his best men to infiltrate the Moors. Their objective was to gather as many of the Tomb Blooms as possible and return—without being caught. Gerda had stiffened at the orders. The last place she wanted to go, especially at night, was the Moors. Every noise sounded suspect; every scent was troubling. She much preferred the clean and orderly Ulstead.

But Ingrith's orders were hers to obey.

Seeing no obvious sign of danger, Percival lowered his hand, and the soldiers moved out of the trees and into a wide-open field. It was full of Tomb Blooms. Hundreds, perhaps even thousands, of the brilliantly colored flowers reached their petals to the moon, which had only now slipped out from behind the clouds. The

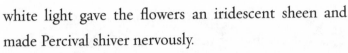

white light gave the flowers an iridescent sheen and made Percival shiver nervously.

He didn't like the light. Darkness was their friend for this mission. Beside him, Ben anxiously swung his gaze back and forth between the dark night sky and the field of Tomb Blooms.

"What if the"—he hesitated, scared even to say the words—"winged one returns?"

Gerda shook her head. "She's gone."

"Are you certain?" the young man pressed.

Gerda didn't answer. She didn't need to. The boy was there to help, not ask questions. But far as she was concerned, Maleficent would never bother them again.

CHAPTER TWELVE

SITTING IN THE CENTRAL CHAMBER OF THE NEST, MALEFICENT, VERY MUCH ALIVE, LOOKED AROUND AT THE DARK FEY GATHERED TOGETHER. THE SIGHT, THOUGH NOW MORE FAMILIAR, STILL MADE HER HEART POUND ODDLY. Spending years alone with the thought that she would never meet another of her kind had made her harder, colder. But now, as she sat drinking and eating with dozens of other Dark Fey around a roaring fire, she felt some of that hardness softening.

Conall sat beside her. He, too, was silent as he listened to the voices ebb and flow around them. Maleficent couldn't help wondering what he was thinking about as he looked around the room. What was he thinking now, as he turned and looked at her? Was he thinking that she seemed lost? Or was he thinking that perhaps here, with them, she was found? His eyes locked on hers, and then slowly he passed her a flagon. She almost laughed at the simple nature of the gesture, which was nothing like the complexity of her thoughts.

She took a sip and then moved to hand it back to him. As she did so, the tips of their wings touched. Instantly, Maleficent pulled her wings back and adjusted on her seat. The sensation of touching someone else was foreign to her. But to her surprise, Conall did not back away.

And then searing pain tore through her. She doubled over as vision after vision bombarded her mind. She could see blades flashing in the air, men slicing through dozens of Tomb Blooms in one fell swoop. She could hear the angry, hurt screams of her kind. Instantly, the softness was gone. Her eyes flashed with fury.

"I have to go," she said.

"What is it?" Conall asked, his voice tinged with worry.

"Humans are in the Moors," she answered. "I feel it." She stood, ready to fly. But Conall blocked her way.

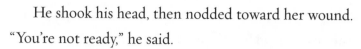

He shook his head, then nodded toward her wound. "You're not ready," he said.

Maleficent was not in the mood. "Move," she snarled.

By this time, the other fey had noticed the anger that flowed from Maleficent's skin. Without her realizing it, green magic was pooling around her feet. Conall ignored them all as he tried in vain to calm her.

"If you go now, you will die," he said matter-of-factly.

"Let her go, Conall." At Borra's voice, Maleficent turned. "Nobody can control her," he said.

Maleficent knew what Borra was doing. It was what he had done since the moment they met: he was goading her, pushing her to release the darkness. She might have fought it before, but not now. More green magic pulsed through her and into the air. "I will not ask again," she said, turning back to Conall.

Tension hung in the air. Then, finally, he moved aside.

Maleficent didn't hesitate. Brushing past him, she spread her wings and lifted from the ground. In moments, she was out of the Nest and flying through the night sky. Her wound ached, but it was no match for the rage that boiled within her. She had left the Moors for only a few days and already they were in danger. Humans. Conall could say all he wanted about the power of love and the ability to change. But those were only words. Actions spoke louder. And right now, the actions of the humans were making her head scream with the voices of her ancestors' anguish.

Hearing wings behind her, she turned, half expecting to see Conall. To her surprise, it was Borra. He didn't say anything as he flew up next to her. But she knew by the look in his eyes why he was there. He was going to help her take down the humans.

In silence, they flew the rest of the distance to the Moors. Swooping down, Maleficent and Borra landed on a large tree branch that looked over the Tomb Bloom clearing—or rather, what *had been* the Tomb Bloom clearing. It was now a scorched tract, stripped bare. Not a single flower remained. All that was left were boot marks in the deep mud.

Maleficent bit back a cry, her heart breaking once again. "This is where we bury our dead," she whispered, explaining the significance to Borra. "They've destroyed it."

Borra looked out at the devastation with a flash in his eyes, then turned to her. His voice was not full of the usual anger Maleficent heard when he spoke. This time, there was another emotion, something that sounded almost like pain. "This is what humans do," he said. "They are nothing but locusts, swarming the earth. We have to stop them." He paused and gestured to the field of nothing. "You spent years caring for a human. Now care for your own."

Maleficent met his gaze. A part of her knew he was right. But another part of her heard Conall, speaking of hope, saying that she and Aurora had shown him another way was possible. Why did it have to be one way or the other? Why couldn't she just find Aurora and leave the other humans alone?

Suddenly, a flock of birds burst into the air.

Maleficent sensed danger and knew the humans

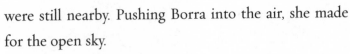

were still nearby. Pushing Borra into the air, she made for the open sky.

"*Fire!*" someone shouted.

Behind the fey, dozens of soldiers, unseen until now, lifted their crossbows. Then they fired. Iron bullets pierced the air. *THWIP-THWIP-THWIP!* The bullets came from above, below, and all around her. She and Borra ducked and weaved, but there were too many soldiers and there was no place to hide.

Time seemed to slow down as Maleficent struggled to stay in the air and away from the iron that would destroy her. She heard Borra screaming and the humans shouting. But something was pulling her back, slowing her down. Weakened by her still healing wound, Maleficent was falling rapidly. She wasn't going to survive this. She knew it. She looked down at the empty field as she stretched her wings and prepared for the inevitable. . . .

Suddenly, powerful arms wrapped around her, and a moment later, wings covered her entire body. Startled, she looked up into the warm, kind eyes of Conall. Time stopped as they hovered in the sky, cocooned together.

And then Conall's body began to convulse as bullet after bullet slammed into him. Maleficent screamed as they fell toward the ground. Maleficent and Conall landed hard and then rolled for a few feet before coming to a stop. Beneath Maleficent, Conall didn't move.

But the soldiers kept coming, their crossbows rearmed, ready to finish them off.

Maleficent raised a hand, and the last of her green magic poured out. Pulling the roots and branches from the ground around them, she formed a protective barrier. The soldiers fired, but the bullets bounced off her shield. With one hand on Conall's chest, Maleficent looked out and watched as Borra let loose the rage he had kept inside.

Soldiers dropped around him one by one as he rampaged. Borra blew some back with his wings while he beat others with tree branches ripped from trunks like they were kindling. Then, with a roar so loud it made a nearly unconscious Conall shiver, Borra went after the last of the men. The ground in front of him opened,

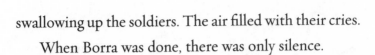

swallowing up the soldiers. The air filled with their cries.

When Borra was done, there was only silence.

The soldiers were gone. Slowly letting the branches and roots pull apart, Maleficent allowed Borra to lift Conall in his arms. Then, together, they began to carry him back to the Nest. Maleficent could do nothing but fly, her eyes trained on the warrior whose face was now ashen, his eyes closed.

The fight, fall, and magic had drained any energy Maleficent had left. But as they flew, one thing kept her wings pumping. It was a vow—a simple one, but one she was going to see through to the end. She was going to make the humans pay. Every last one of them.

On one of the castle's guard towers, Queen Ingrith stood waiting. She was making her own vows. Vows to destroy. Vows to take power. Vows she made nearly every evening. Only now, she could finally see them through.

Hearing a commotion, she looked down and saw a line of soldiers approaching the castle. She could see, even from a distance, that the large brown sacks they

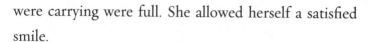

were carrying were full. She allowed herself a satisfied smile.

The sound of boots on stone alerted her to the presence of Gerda and Percival, who had come ahead of the others. Turning, she waited for them to make their report. Their faces were smeared with dirt, and their clothes were a mess, but they looked pleased. "We've got them," Gerda said as she approached. "Over a thousand blooms!"

"Maleficent was there, Your Majesty," Percival added, earning himself a stern glare from Gerda. "She was in the Moors with two others. One of them sacrificed himself for her."

"One creature saved another?" Ingrith asked.

Percival nodded.

Interesting, she thought. She had not foreseen that. She had anticipated that the Dark Fey would look after only themselves, the way Maleficent had looked after only herself when she abandoned Aurora in Ulstead. Ingrith shrugged. No matter. It wouldn't change anything.

"Iron or no iron," Percival went on, "they will be coming for us."

Leaving her perch, Ingrith joined Gerda and Percival in the castle's main gate. Once there, she slowly picked up a Tomb Bloom with her gloved hand. She ran a finger gently along the petal. "One can only hope," she said.

"Mother?"

Hearing Phillip's voice, Ingrith startled. The Tomb Bloom dropped to the ground. He was standing with his arms crossed, looking back and forth between her and the soldiers.

"What is all this?" he asked.

Swallowing, Ingrith took off her glove and picked up the Tomb Bloom. The pain was instant as her flesh touched the flower, but she bit back a cry and held it out to her son. "It was going to be a surprise," she said. "Real flowers for your wedding."

"Flowers?" Phillip repeated. "Won't they make you ill?"

Ingrith felt small beads of sweat pooling at her hairline as she continued to hold the offending flower. "A small sacrifice for Aurora. She deserves it," Ingrith lied. She had to make her son believe all was well. Ingrith thrust the flower into his hand and quickly put her glove back on. Immediately, she felt her heart begin to slow and the sweat subside. "Get some rest now," she said, ushering Phillip back inside the castle. "In a few hours, it will all be over."

As he disappeared through the doors, Ingrith looked back at the Tomb Blooms and smiled to herself sinisterly. Indeed, in a few hours it *would* all be over—for the faeries.

CHAPTER THIRTEEN

MALEFICENT WATCHED AS BORRA SLOWLY LOWERED CONALL TO THE GROUND IN FRONT OF THE GREAT TREE. THEY HAD ARRIVED BACK AT THE NEST NOT A MOMENT TOO SOON. Conall's breathing was shallow and his face pale. Blood oozed from dozens of wounds and pooled beneath him. The sight made Maleficent sick with guilt.

The tree seemed to react to Conall's pain and Maleficent's grief. Its leaves drooped, and its bark began to drip, as though it were shedding tears. The deep roots lifted, creating a cradle around the Dark Fey as he lay motionless.

News of what had happened quickly spread, and the chamber grew crowded as the other fey gathered. Their voices were hushed as they talked among themselves.

Maleficent overheard bits and pieces of conversations. "Humans." "Iron bullets." "Surprise attack." And the worst of it: "Sacrifice."

Maleficent looked down at Conall, trying to calm her racing heart. It wasn't right. It wasn't fair. She had not asked him to sacrifice his life for hers, yet it was almost as if she had known that he would be there. That their destiny had been written long before. But it still seemed wrong. She had only just found Conall. Now she was going to lose him—forever.

Hearing a sniffle beside her, Maleficent turned to look. A young fey, one she had watched learn to fly, had come to stand beside her. The young one was openly crying as she gingerly reached out to touch one of Conall's many wounds. Seeing her own pain mirrored in the girl's face, Maleficent carefully wrapped her arms around the young fey. The girl turned her head into Maleficent's shoulder and let the tears fall. Covering the girl with her wings, Maleficent slowly rubbed the girl's head as, together, they grieved.

Lost in the moment, Maleficent didn't notice Borra's

eyes on her as she comforted the girl. Her anger was still there, simmering close to the surface as she stood under the heavy leaves of the Great Tree beside a dying Conall. But she did not need to show Borra that. He knew. Conall's sacrifice did not just impact her. It impacted the whole Nest. And when he was gone, he would leave an impossibly large hole.

Diaval didn't like this. He didn't like the Moors without Maleficent, he didn't like being trapped in human form, and he certainly didn't like being forced to leave the Moors—again—to attend Aurora's wedding. As far as he was concerned, she should be getting married in her own castle among her own people, not across the river in the cold of Castle Ulstead.

And yet here he was, following a long procession of Moor folk as they made their way through the Moors. The sun was just rising over the horizon, lighting the Moors in brilliant reds, oranges, and pinks. Diaval looked up. The sky was cloudless; it was the perfect day for a wedding. Still, he couldn't shake the feeling that a storm was coming, and it made him uneasy. He snapped at a mushroom faerie as it moved past him, nearly tripping him.

Ahead, Lief, Aurora's tree advisor, came to a stop at the border. Knotgrass fluttered nervously about, trying to keep order. "Everyone stay together!" she called. "We're about to leave the Moors."

"Grab the hand or the wing or the tail of whoever is closest to you," Flittle added.

Satisfied that they were ready, Lief growled and then stepped over the border. For the first time in a long time, he, and almost every faerie behind him, left the Moors and entered the realm of the humans.

As Knotgrass, Flittle, and Thistlewit flew around him, Diaval kept his head down. The feeling in his stomach grew stronger the closer they got to Ulstead Castle. He saw colorful banners flapping in the breeze and heard bells ringing joyfully, but Diaval remained wary. They were, in his opinion, entering enemy territory. And without Maleficent, they were doing so without a true guardian.

Approaching the main gate, Diaval spotted a line of heavily armed soldiers. It was odd in contrast to the otherwise festive atmosphere, and he picked up his pace so as not to spend too much time near them. Ahead, guards were directing wedding attendees. There were two lines. The humans, a hodgepodge of nobles and commoners, were being directed one way, while the Moor folk were told to go directly into the chapel.

As Diaval got closer to the chapel, a soldier stopped him.

"Oh, I'm with the bride," Diaval said.

To his surprise, the soldier pulled him out of the line. "We've been asked to let the, er, other kind," he said, gesturing at the Moor folk, "find their seats first."

For a split second, Diaval was confused. What did the soldier mean? Then it clicked. To the soldier, Diaval looked like a human. He silently cursed Maleficent for leaving him in this horrific state. "Actually, I'm a raven," he said, trying to clear things up.

This time it was the soldier who looked confused. "A what?" he asked.

"A small black bird. About yea big," Diaval said, moving his hands about eight inches apart.

The soldier shrugged, not sure what to think. But the line behind them was growing. Impatiently, he pushed Diaval over to stand with the humans and told him to wait. Then he turned back to the Moor folk and continued to usher them into the chapel.

"We should be seated first," a nearby nobleman muttered. "I don't understand. Why do we have to wait for them?"

As other humans voiced their displeasure with being told to wait, Diaval listened and watched. The bad feeling in his stomach worsened. Something was wrong. But what? Why were they separating the Moor folk from the humans? Taking advantage of the distraction, Diaval backed away and slipped out of sight.

He didn't have wings to help him, but he still had his eyes and ears. He could use them to figure out the meaning of all this. . . .

• • •

Aurora barely registered the fanfare outside her chamber walls. She didn't hear the ringing bells or the small din created by the hundreds of guests who began arriving before the sun rose. It was her wedding day, and she was already exhausted.

She'd spent an almost sleepless night with Diaval's words echoing in her head. What if Maleficent was *not* to blame for the king's condition? If not Maleficent, who could have done such a thing? When she tried to stop thinking and closed her eyes, images of Maleficent flashed through her mind. When sleep finally came, her dreams were plagued by visions of horns and green magic and even greener eyes. She finally gave up on getting any rest and spent the remainder of the long night pacing her chambers, coming to one simple conclusion: something was wrong. She knew it. But she didn't know what it was. Or what to do.

Now she stood staring at Queen Ingrith's—or rather, her—wedding dress. It hung in front of her, the ornate patterns seeming to shift and change as the sun caught the beading through the window. Her eyes turned from that dress to the one she'd brought from the Moors. In contrast, it was simple, with no beading or jewels. Her fingers itched to put it on instead of Ingrith's. Hearing a gentle knock at the door, she turned to see Phillip entering. She shook her head.

"I know, I know. It's bad luck," he said, reading her face. "But I had to see you." He held out a flower.

Aurora was no longer listening. Her eyes were glued to the flower. Reaching out, she took it from him. Maleficent had taught her long before the great importance of the Tomb Blooms. They were never to be taken from the ground—or the Moors. "A Tomb Bloom? Where did you get it?" she asked.

He looked down at the flower and then back at her and shrugged. "It was a gift—from my mother."

When Aurora did not say anything, Phillip gave her a quick kiss on the top of her head and turned to go, unaware that his fiancée's brain was spinning. "The sun is up, Aurora. It's our wedding day." With those parting words, he left.

Aurora stood there for a long time once Phillip was gone, her fingers trembling as she held the sacred flower. There was no reason Ingrith should have a Tomb Bloom. It didn't make sense.

Quickly, Aurora walked out of her room. She needed to find Ingrith. Perhaps the queen had a reasonable explanation for taking such a treasure from the Moors. But as Aurora walked, she couldn't help worrying that this sinking, unsettling feeling had something to do with Ingrith herself.

CHAPTER FOURTEEN

AURORA WAS GLAD, FOR ONCE, FOR THE COMMOTION THE WEDDING WAS CAUSING. WITH EVERYONE BUSY PREPARING FOR THE EVENT, SHE WAS ABLE TO SLIP THROUGH THE HALLS OF THE CASTLE UNNOTICED. She made her way to the queen's room and knocked. When no one answered, she carefully opened the door and slid inside.

The room was dark and silent. Ingrith must have already dressed and left. Slowly, Aurora wandered around the room, looking. She wasn't sure exactly what she was looking for—a pile of Tomb Blooms, a diary detailing Ingrith's thoughts . . . Whatever it was, she didn't see it. So she moved farther into the room, entering the huge closet. The life-size dress forms stood in front of her, looking ominous in the dim light.

Suddenly, a loud whisper filled the room. Aurora's

eyes widened as the tip of her finger began to ache. Looking down, she saw that her scar, the physical reminder of when she had pricked her finger and fallen under Maleficent's curse, was bright red.

What was happening?

The whisper in her head got louder as she walked closer to the dress forms. It was a sound both familiar and foreign. Closing her eyes, she allowed the whisper to pull her forward, past the dress forms and against the back wall of the closet. The dress form nearest her fell with a thud as she pushed the wall. The whisper got louder, more frantic. She pushed harder until she heard a click. Then a secret door opened, revealing a hidden staircase.

Finger throbbing and head full of whispers, Aurora moved through the door and down the steps. She felt as though her body was being controlled by something—or someone—else. It was as though she were a puppet, with her feet moved up and down by invisible strings. As she reached the bottom of the stairs, the whisper grew still louder. Now it was almost a scream. The noise blotted out everything else. She didn't even notice the jars full of faeries or the small man standing near them, shouting at her.

All she could hear was the whisper; all she could feel was her scar, pulling her forward. Moving through the lab, she didn't stop until she was in the middle of an alcove. And there, in front of her, its spindle gleaming wickedly in the light from a dozen candles, was the spinning wheel.

The whispers stopped.

The trance broken, Aurora looked down at the spinning wheel. Carefully, she reached out and pulled it from the small dark room. In the brighter light of the lab, the spinning wheel reflected Aurora's astonished expression.

Why was the spinning wheel *here* . . . in Castle Ulstead?

And then, in a flash, Aurora understood.

She saw the fateful dinner. She heard Ingrith taunting Maleficent, goading her to anger as she talked about Aurora's moving to Ulstead and becoming the daughter

Ingrith had never had. She felt Maleficent's anger and watched as magic began to pool around the Dark Fey, causing Ingrith to cling to her husband in fear.

But now she saw the truth, too. Ingrith felt no fear. She had no desire to make Aurora a part of her life. Those were just words to anger Maleficent so that Ingrith could carry out her plan. And she had done it brilliantly. No one thought to look closely as the queen cowered beside her husband, her face pale and her hands shaking. No one thought to check whether her long sleeves hid anything suspect. And no one noticed that at the very same moment King John winced in pain, the tip of the spindle flashed brightly before disappearing into Ingrith's sleeve once more.

Everyone was focused on Maleficent, her green magic, the terrifying stories about her, and the mistake she had made years earlier.

It had been the perfect misdirection.

And Aurora, just like everyone else, had fallen for it, hook, line, and spindle. As the images faded from her mind, Aurora let out a cry of anguish and dropped to her knees. Grief overwhelmed her. She had begged Maleficent to fix King John when the Dark Fey had been innocent. She had turned her back on Maleficent, just like her father, King Stefan, had done years earlier. She had proven to Maleficent that humans were exactly as she thought—cold, cruel, and fickle.

What had she done?

No. What had Ingrith *made* her do?

Something powerful cut through Aurora's anger. It was resolve. With renewed focus, Aurora looked up to find Lickspittle running toward her, waving his arms and yelling at her to get out. Her eyes narrowed as she finally took in her surroundings.

What *was* this place?

She saw rows of jars behind the small man. And in each jar was a faerie. "Stolen faeries!" she said in shock. Then she looked back at the man and her confusion grew. "And you—you're a pixie!"

The man sneered. "How dare you call me such a thing!"

Ignoring his protests, Aurora reached out and lifted

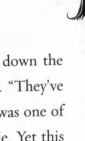

the back of his shirt. Two parallel scars ran down the length of his back, a reminder of his wings. "They've taken your wings," Aurora said, horrified. It was one of the worst things a human could do to a faerie. Yet this pixie seemed to be working for Ingrith. "What's your name, pixie?"

"It's . . . Lickspittle," the man finally said. "And I am no pixie. I am a nobleman!"

Aurora felt strangely sorry for the creature. The queen had taken his wings, kept him prisoner down here. And yet he continued to work for her, betraying his own kind to do so. She had to wonder, why?

As if reading her thoughts, Lickspittle continued. "She promised me—when every last faerie is gone, I am free to go."

"Gone?" She repeated the word, which felt like poison on her tongue. "But we have to release them!" She inched closer, holding out her hand. Her eyes pleaded with him as she gestured to all the other faeries, trapped in jars. They didn't deserve this. "They belong to the Moors."

"As do you, Aurora. . . ."

Ingrith's voice was unmistakable. Aurora turned and watched as Ingrith stepped into the dim light. Her eyes were as cold as her voice as she continued to speak. "A human. Who has betrayed her own kind." Behind Ingrith were two heavily armed soldiers, their hands resting on swords, and crossbows fastened on their backs.

"You!" Aurora said. "*You* put the curse on the king."

If she had expected a weepy confession and admission of great and terrible guilt, she did not get it.

"He served his purpose," the queen replied coldly.

"How could you?" Aurora gasped. An image of the king, his body motionless on his bed while Phillip stood grieving beside him, flashed through her mind. She looked over at the icy woman in disbelief.

Ingrith ignored the look. Instead, she moved through the room, her fingers trailing over the jars and lingering on a bubbling vial. "You may be queen, but you are very young. Ruling humans is a bit more complicated than running around barefoot with flowers in your hair."

Aurora opened her mouth to protest but a sharp look from Ingrith silenced her.

The queen went on. Her voice grew deeper as she told Aurora her story. "When I was young, my family's kingdom bordered the Moors. One particularly harsh winter, our crops died and the people began to suffer the same fate. As we looked across our walls, we could see the faeries thriving." At the mention of the creatures, Ingrith's lips pulled back in a sneer. "My brother and I believed we should take what we needed—deserved—while my father, the king, sought their kindness. Choosing peace over our people, he sent my brother to do his bidding." She paused in front of a jar. Inside, the trapped faerie frantically backed away. But it had nowhere to go. Ingrith smiled cruelly and went on. "Those savages—creatures who could barely grunt let alone engage in talks—killed him."

Aurora shook her head. "I don't believe that."

Ingrith ignored her. "Our people became fearful. They overthrew my father, and the land fell into chaos.

I was cast out—forced by fate into a marriage with King John of Ulstead, another weak king speaking of tolerance and civility." By her sides, Ingrith's hands clenched, turning even paler than normal. Her hard gaze landed once more on Aurora. "And now my own son corrupted by visions of harmony! But 'peace' will not be our downfall."

The queen moved closer to Aurora, and Aurora instinctually stepped back. Smoothing her hands down the front of her dress, Ingrith composed herself. The spark of anger she had shown was gone. Once more, she was ice and stone. "I'm doing what the men before me could not do," she said. "Because sometimes, it takes a woman's touch." Turning to go, she nodded at the soldiers. "Now lock her up. There is a war coming."

Before Aurora could move, the soldiers were upon her. Grabbing her arms, they dragged her out of the lab. Behind her, she saw the faeries—her people—banging helplessly against the jars, trying to save their queen. And now she couldn't do anything to save them, either.

As the door to her chambers slammed and locked, Aurora looked out on the castle grounds far, far below. She was trapped.

And Ingrith was free, to destroy faerie kind—forever.

Oh, Maleficent, where are you? Aurora thought as she banged her fists uselessly on the locked door. It was pointless. No one would hear her cries for help. Ingrith had seen to that. Aurora angrily hit the door again. Why hadn't Maleficent come back? Aurora couldn't do this on her own. She couldn't watch everyone she loved be destroyed, but without Maleficent, how could she stop Ingrith?

Her sobs echoed through the chamber as she gave in to her agony. The day that was supposed to be the happiest in her life, her wedding day, was now the worst.

Inside King John's chambers, Phillip sat, staring at his father's still body. The room was dark. Thick curtains had been pulled across the windows (by order of the queen), blocking all light and sound. In the shadowy gray, the huge trophy heads on the wall loomed larger and more frightening. They seemed to look down on the king, as if amused to see the man who had brought their lives to an end clinging now to his very own.

Phillip gingerly lifted his father's hand and placed it in his own. It looked frail, the veins visible beneath his skin. All his years, Phillip had thought of his father as unstoppable. The king had taken such joy in life. In many ways, King John made up for Ingrith's cold demeanor. He had been the bighearted parent. He had been present at every important moment of Phillip's life—from his first steps, to the first time he rode a horse, to the day he came home with his first victory at battle. And now he was going to miss the most important one of all.

"All I want is for you to be here with me," Phillip said softly, his voice heavy with emotion. He paused, as if by some miracle the man's eyes might open and he might say, "Why, of course, Son. Wouldn't miss it for the world." But the king remained silent.

Phillip would have to do this on his own. He rose

to his feet. "I hope I make you proud," he said. Then he turned and picked up the sword that was laid across a nearby table. Placing it in the scabbard, he moved to go.

Shaking his head, Phillip moved toward the door. It was foolish to play out impossible scenarios. It didn't change the fact that he was about to get married without the presence of his father.

CHAPTER FIFTEEN

CONALL WAS DYING.

MALEFICENT HAD NOT MOVED FROM HIS SIDE SINCE THEY HAD PLACED HIM BESIDE THE GREAT TREE. SHE HAD REMAINED AS HE THRASHED IN PAIN, AS HIS BODY HAD FINALLY STILLED, AND EVEN NOW AS HE STRUGGLED TO BRING AIR INTO HIS CHEST.

Slowly, as the other fey formed a circle around them, Maleficent put her hand on Conall's chest. She heard Borra's low voice and the sound of footsteps as he and the other warriors moved outside the sacred chamber. She tried not to listen as they spoke, but her ears were too keen, their voices not quite soft enough.

"Conall wanted peace," Borra was saying. Maleficent couldn't see him, but she imagined his eyes were red with rage. "And they filled him with iron. Now we will have our war. Our fight begins now."

As the others joined in his cry, Maleficent's fingers tensed. This wasn't what Conall would have wanted. Not even in his dying moments. He was kind, forgiving, willing to see another way. She knew that. But Maleficent was conflicted. She also knew that Borra wasn't wrong. The humans were killing them. Should they stand idly by and let it happen?

"Today the human empire will fall!" Borra went on. "And we will show them *no mercy*!" As his cry faded, the sound of flapping wings filled the chamber. The warriors were leaving.

It was time to bring the fight to Ingrith and the humans.

Ingrith was pleased. At long last, after all her planning and plotting, she was going to exact her revenge against the faeries. All the obstacles were out of the way. Per her instructions, Aurora was locked in her chambers and the entire population of the Moors was, at that very moment, being locked inside the chapel. Thanks

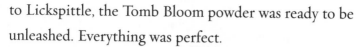

to Lickspittle, the Tomb Bloom powder was ready to be unleashed. Everything was perfect.

Even when Percival informed her that there was a group of Dark Fey approaching, Ingrith remained unbothered. Let them come. They would be no match for the red dust. Large fey or small faerie, the red dust would simply destroy.

From inside her tower, she heard organ music play. Her smile widened. She could see it now. Gerda must have taken her place at the large instrument that dominated the far wall of the chapel. Behind her, the faeries would have taken their seats, eager to see their queen walk down the aisle. But little did they know that this was the beginning of a massacre—not a wedding.

It had been her idea—and a brilliant one, she thought—to have Lickspittle's red dust placed inside the large organ pipes. As Gerda began to play, the red dust—made from Tomb Blooms—would be pulled up through the pipes and then pumped out into the air, destroying every last one of those despicable creatures from the Moors.

As the music became more intense, Ingrith nodded with satisfaction. There was no escaping her trap now. She knew that the red dust had begun to drift down the aisles. She relished the notion that as the dust touched the faeries, they would start to transform, one by one, until there was nothing left but a chapel of inanimate remains.

The massacre was underway. Ingrith had done it. She had won.

Aurora pounded on the window of her chamber. She watched as the last of the faeries marched into the chapel far below. She saw the guards barricade the heavy doors, making it impossible for the faerie folk to leave. Once more, she slammed her fists against the glass, trying to get anyone's attention. But it was in vain. No one could hear her. And the guards standing outside her door had been ordered to ignore her cries.

Her hands stilled on the glass as she dropped her

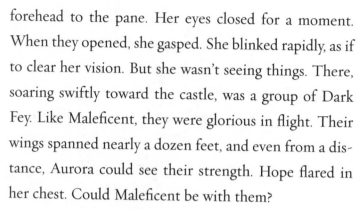

forehead to the pane. Her eyes closed for a moment. When they opened, she gasped. She blinked rapidly, as if to clear her vision. But she wasn't seeing things. There, soaring swiftly toward the castle, was a group of Dark Fey. Like Maleficent, they were glorious in flight. Their wings spanned nearly a dozen feet, and even from a distance, Aurora could see their strength. Hope flared in her chest. Could Maleficent be with them?

With renewed determination, Aurora paced back and forth. The Dark Fey were powerful. But they couldn't defeat Ingrith on their own. She had to help them stop Ingrith and save her people. But how?

Then her eyes landed on the long train of Ingrith's wedding dress—the one Aurora was supposed to wear that day. It was still on the dress form, and an idea began to take shape. Aurora moved toward the dress, lifting the train in her hands and tugging at it. The fabric was strong. It could work. . . .

She raced to the bed, pulled off the linens, and began to tie them together. When she ran out of sheets, she tied the ends to the wedding dress train. Tying that to the bedpost, she paused, eyeing the now extensive length of homemade rope. *I'm sure this is not what Ingrith had in mind when she gave me her dress,* Aurora thought, allowing herself a small smile.

Satisfied that everything was in order, Aurora dragged the rope to the window. Using the sheets to protect her hand, she beat her fist against the glass over and over until the window broke with a loud smash. As glass shattered and fell to the floor, Aurora threw the rope out the window and let it dangle. Then she ran back toward the door to her room.

A moment later, just as she had anticipated, the guards rushed in. Spotting the rope, they raced to the window and looked out. They assumed that Aurora had climbed out and escaped. But they were wrong. Distracted by the broken window and wedding dress rope, they didn't notice Aurora slipping through the open door. They were confused about Aurora's whereabouts until they heard the door slam and the lock click into place.

Now *they* were trapped and Aurora was free.

But not for long. Racing down the long hallway, she spotted four more guards moving toward her. Her head spun as she looked for an escape. It seemed her only option was another window. Through an open pane, she could see her makeshift rope hanging. Taking a deep breath, she ran—and jumped. Her legs and arms pumped in the air as she reached for the rope. Her fingers connected with the fabric, and she clutched it as she dangled for a moment, her body swaying back and forth. Above, she heard a loud screech as the bed, which the rope was still tied to, began to move, pulled forward by her weight.

The screeching got louder. Aurora gulped. It was only a matter of time before the bed would slide across the room. And when it crashed against the wall, she was going to plummet to her death. Frantically, Aurora began to pump her legs, swinging her body like a pendulum.

She dropped farther as the bed slid a few more feet across the room. Now she was dangling in front of another window. If she didn't figure out a way off the rope soon, she would die. She heard the organ playing

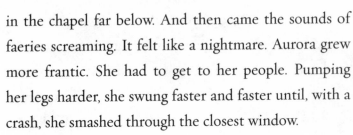

in the chapel far below. And then came the sounds of faeries screaming. It felt like a nightmare. Aurora grew more frantic. She had to get to her people. Pumping her legs harder, she swung faster and faster until, with a crash, she smashed through the closest window.

Her feet landed on the carpeted floor of the king's royal chambers. As she tried to catch her balance, her arms thrashed wildly. She was just about to fall back out the window when a hand reached out and steadied her. Looking up, she found herself staring into Phillip's warm eyes.

"What's going on?" he asked.

Aurora didn't get a chance to answer. A loud boom rocked the room. Looking out the broken window, she saw the Dark Fey approaching the castle. They swooped and dove through the air as Percival and a dozen other soldiers fired at them from the queen's tower.

For a moment, Aurora was speechless. She had never before seen anything so beautiful in her life. The Dark Fey looked like huge birds of myth with their wings outstretched. Some were brilliantly colored, while others were duller, more the colors of sand and stone. Some had large horns, while others' were smaller, tighter to their heads. But all of them had one thing in common. "They look just like her," Aurora said, finally finding her voice. Scanning the sky, she strained to see if her godmother was among them. But Aurora did not see Maleficent. Her chest heaved.

Phillip had been silent, too, as he watched the Dark Fey come closer. He pointed at the winged creatures. "Maleficent is starting a war!" he cried. "First my father, and now this."

Aurora heard the anguish in Phillip's voice and felt for him, but he was wrong. She didn't say anything but simply looked on as Percival's soldiers fired more crossbows. The ammunition, which she couldn't quite make out, appeared to be a red shell of sorts. It flew and slammed into one of the fey. In horror, she watched as the Dark Fey exploded, transforming from a solid shape into water. Then another fey was hit, and turned to dust.

Ingrith's weapon. This had to be it. Aurora's face paled as she once again remembered the Tomb Bloom

Phillip had held in his hand. He'd said Ingrith had given it to him. She must have weaponized the flowers and was now using the red powder against the faeries and the Dark Fey. As the Dark Fey began to break formation, some diving toward the center of the town, while others tried to get closer to the queen's tower, Aurora turned from the window. She saw that Phillip was moving to leave, eager to stop the war he did not understand.

"It's not Maleficent," Aurora said, finally giving voice to her thoughts. "Phillip, she never cursed him. It was your mother. I'm sorry."

Phillip opened his mouth to protest but stopped as he heard more screams from outside. His shoulders sagged. "What are you saying?" he asked softly, as if he knew the answer but needed to hear it anyway.

"It was the spindle," Aurora said, her heart aching as she watched Phillip's face fall. "The curse is still in it." With the sounds of war still waging outside, Aurora moved into the center of the chamber, to where King John lay on his bed. Gently, she lifted his arm and pulled back his sleeve. "Your mother used it against your father. Look," she said, nodding to the small, barely noticeable red mark on the king's upper arm.

Phillip's eyes grew wide in pained understanding. "They're the same," he said.

Aurora could do nothing but nod. She saw Phillip's thoughts play out on his face as he moved from disbelief to anger to grief and back to anger. She didn't want him to hurt, but she needed him by her side. Now more than ever. Pulling him back to the window, Aurora pointed to the chapel far below. "She's locked the Moor folk inside!" Her voice became more frantic as she thought about what was happening—probably at that very moment— to her people. "This isn't a wedding." She stared into Phillip's eyes, willing him to believe. "It's a trap."

Slowly, Phillip reached out his hand and squeezed Aurora's. Her breath hitched. "We have to stop her," he said.

Aurora exhaled. Then she gave Phillip a determined nod. "Go!" she said. She didn't have to tell him where.

He knew. He had to find his mother. "I'm going to the chapel."

Together, they rushed for the door. All Aurora could do now was hope they weren't too late.

CHAPTER SIXTEEN

THERE WASN'T MUCH TIME LEFT. MALEFICENT KNEW THAT AS SHE LOOKED DOWN AT CONALL. HIS BODY WAS FADING, HIS BREATHING MORE RAGGED. For a few brief moments, he seemed to rally, and Maleficent allowed herself the smallest sliver of hope that perhaps he would surprise them all and fight through the wounds.

But then he weakened again. The others, sensing the end was close, said their good-byes and left Maleficent and Conall alone. The room was silent now and oddly cozy—despite the fact that Conall lay dying in front of the Great Tree.

Maleficent wasn't sure what to do or what to say. But then she thought of Aurora, who had always encouraged her to speak her mind—and her heart. She could keep her emotions inside as she had always done, but what good would that do? How would that help Conall in his last moments? Breathing deep, she knelt down and took Conall's hand in hers. Honesty it would be. "You saved my life . . . twice," she said, surprised to hear her voice crack with emotion.

Conall's mouth opened as he tried to find the breath and energy to speak. Seeing him struggle, Maleficent felt her eyes fill with tears. It was hard to believe that only days earlier, he had been a vision of strength. But while his body was weak, there was still strength in his eyes as he looked at her now. "Remember where you came from," he said. "I have made my choice. You must make yours."

Why? Maleficent wanted to cry. *Why did you make the choice to save me?* But those words wouldn't come. "I don't want you to die," she said instead.

"This was always my time," Conall said. "It's only death." As he spoke, he struggled to sit up. Reaching out, he cradled Maleficent's face in his hands, gently rubbing her tearstained cheek with his thumb.

Pulling back, she eased Conall down as the last

breath left his body. As it did, a blue light began to pulse from him, filling the air between them. Gasping in surprise, Maleficent inhaled the light.

The sensation was immediate. The wound in her stomach vanished as Conall's spirit was absorbed into her body and began to spread. She felt new strength fill her muscles, and her wings extended wide, pulsating with power. Looking down, she saw green magic pooling at her fingertips, vibrating and pulsing, ready and waiting to be unleashed. Getting to her feet, Maleficent stretched, and then her eyes widened.

Like her, the Great Tree was absorbing Conall's spirit. It was like the Tomb Blooms in the Moors, she realized. A connection between the living and the dead, a holder of all the magic fey who had passed from this world to the next. As she watched, the tree grew a new branch. Vibrant green leaves budded and matured until they were thick. Reaching out like an arm, the branch covered Conall until he faded from sight. Moments later, when the branch lifted, Conall was gone. He had become part of the tree. He was finally at peace.

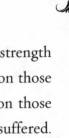

Maleficent, however, was not. With her new strength came new rage. She wanted revenge. Revenge on those who had taken Conall from her and revenge on those who stood for all the sadness the Dark Fey had suffered. And now, with her strength returned, she would exact that revenge no matter what the cost.

Glancing one last time at the Great Tree, Maleficent squared her shoulders, and then, spreading her wings, she flew.

Ingrith was thrilled.

Standing in her tower, she watched through her telescope as half a dozen Dark Fey ducked and weaved, trying to evade the red shells her soldiers fired with abandon. Shouting to his warriors, the leader of the fey indicated for them to dive. They swooped down to the river and then skimmed along its surface before streaking up the face of the castle. Close to the stone wall, the soldiers were unable to get clean shots, so the fey were able to fly safely.

Or so they thought.

Ingrith smiled gleefully as the first of them flew right into her trap.

Pumping their wings, they skimmed along the wall until they reached the top. A line of decorative kites flapped in the breeze in front of them. Spotting the harmless decoration, the fey moved toward the kites.

Ingrith held her breath, waiting as they flew closer. And closer. And closer still. When they were almost upon the kites, Ingrith shouted, "Ignite!"

At her command, the soldiers fired—directly at the kites. In an instant, fuses hidden until then burst into flame. The kites turned from harmless decoration to clouds of red dust. As Ingrith watched in delight, four of the fey flew right into the dust. Immediately, they burst into water, sand, and ice. The leader barely avoided the dust himself. Letting out a scream of rage, he went at the soldiers.

But it didn't matter. Not now. Ingrith had gotten exactly what she wanted. It was a massacre.

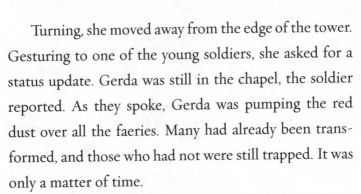

Turning, she moved away from the edge of the tower. Gesturing to one of the young soldiers, she asked for a status update. Gerda was still in the chapel, the soldier reported. As they spoke, Gerda was pumping the red dust over all the faeries. Many had already been transformed, and those who had not were still trapped. It was only a matter of time.

"Mother—" The sound of Phillip's voice over the barrage of red dust surprised Ingrith. She turned and saw him standing on the other side of the tower, his hands clenched by his sides, his face a mask of disappointment and anger. "You need to stop this," he said.

Ingrith shook her head. "We are at war," she said.

"This isn't a war!" Phillip snapped, all traces of patience and kindness gone from his voice. "It's a massacre!"

If the venom hadn't been targeted at her, Ingrith would have been impressed by Phillip's sudden backbone. But right now, she didn't have time for his righteousness. She needed him to understand. "These creatures stand between us and everything we deserve," she said. "Ulstead will never flourish while they are alive . . . while they have what we do not. I am protecting the kingdom—and your future."

Phillip's eyes narrowed at her words. "What about my father? Were you protecting him?"

Ingrith bit back a snarl. Her son's sudden show of strength had come at the most inopportune time, and she was done with it. Turning to Percival, who had silently been watching the mother and son, she gestured to Phillip. "The prince isn't feeling well. See him to his chambers."

With her command issued, Ingrith turned her attention back to the sky. Behind her, Percival hesitated, unsure what to do. Before he could do anything, Phillip acted. Racing to the edge of the tower, the prince leapt. Ingrith's head whipped around as she watched her son's body hover in mid-air for a moment. A cry started in her throat but stopped as she watched Phillip's long arms reach out and snag the string of a passing kite. Torn free from the ramparts, it was floating up into the sky. But with Phillip's weight it began to fall.

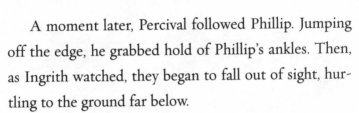

A moment later, Percival followed Phillip. Jumping off the edge, he grabbed hold of Phillip's ankles. Then, as Ingrith watched, they began to fall out of sight, hurtling to the ground far below.

Ingrith sensed the other soldiers' eyes on her, but she did not give them the satisfaction of a reaction. She couldn't afford to back down. Not now, when victory was so close. Phillip had chosen the wrong day to become a man. As the soldiers grabbed Aurora and dragged her away from the chapel below, Ingrith watched Phillip and Percival's fight take them toward the lawn. She let him go.

But as her gaze moved over the tower, she saw something—or rather, someone—on the horizon. A cloud of flashing green lightning was growing. Ingrith's smile of victory faltered.

Maleficent was coming. . . .

CHAPTER SEVENTEEN

Diaval struggled against the ropes that bound his hands. The thick twine dug into his flesh, causing it to sting and burn. But he barely registered the pain. He was too focused on the soldiers standing guard over him, their fingers resting on their weapons. They stared back at him, taking pleasure in what they thought was his pain.

After slipping out of the human line, Diaval had managed to evade the guards and soldiers long enough to make it to the chapel. His eyes widened in terror as he watched red dust, created from the Tomb Blooms that had once marked the faeries' graves in the Moors, drift down over the trapped faerie folk. Every faerie it touched was instantly transformed into their "natural" form. Mushroom faeries became simple fungus. Dandelion faeries turned to flowers, while tree faeries grew stiff, their legs becoming roots that dug into the chapel floor. In horror, Diaval had even watched Flittle, the sweet and huge-hearted pixie, transformed into a flower bush as she tried to save the others. It had been traumatizing.

And then Aurora had arrived, and hope had flared.

"Aurora . . ." Diaval said, grabbing the girl and pulling her into a tight hug. He felt her thin arms wrap tightly around him and for a moment, they just clung to each other, as on the other side of the door, the faeries screamed out for help.

"We need to get them out," she cried, pulling free. Frantically, she began to tug at the door.

Distracted, Diaval didn't hear the soldiers until it was too late. Rough hands grabbed at him, pulling him back and away from Aurora.

"Unhand him!" Aurora cried.

In response, another pair of soldiers grabbed her.

Diaval thrashed and struggled. But it was no use. In a flash, the soldiers threw themselves on him. Their heavy, smelly bodies covered him as he flailed about, trying to find freedom and fresh air. The soldiers' uniforms and the flash of metal from their weapons surrounded him.

Suddenly, a loud bellow broke through the din of the soldiers' attack. To Diaval's surprise, the noise was coming from him. Looking down, he saw that he no longer had the weak, long-fingered hands of a human but the massive pads of a black bear. Letting out another roar, he rose on all fours. The soldiers went flying as Diaval began to bat them away like they were nothing more than bugs.

Diaval heard more screaming behind him. And he knew why. His transformation had made it clear enough, but Aurora's words confirmed it.

As Aurora looked up at the sky, a smile broke over her frightened face. "Maleficent," she said.

Diaval reared back and let out another roar. Everyone *was* going to pay.

Turning, he shook off the last of the soldiers and then slammed into the chapel doors. The wood splintered as easily as a toothpick. The faerie folk who had escaped the transformation began to stream out of the chapel and race to safety. Diaval would make sure they were safe. She was sure of that. But it was up to Maleficent to take care of the rest.

Maleficent's giant wings flapped powerfully as she flew closer to Ulstead. The rage that had begun as she watched Conall's life fade had strengthened during her journey over the water. Now, as she arrived at the border to the kingdom, she was seething. Green magic burst from her in powerful shock waves, knocking down anything and anyone that fell in its path.

Getting closer, she waved her hands, opening a huge hole in the earth in front of the castle. Soldiers standing guard fell into the abyss with screams. Another wave of her fingers and a tornado dropped from the sky, sucking up still more soldiers. In vain, the men fired at her, trying to take her down. But Maleficent was too high and too fast. She easily evaded them.

As the parapets came into view, gleaming white, she laughed at the irony. The queen who called the palace her home had a heart that was dark and smoldering—the furthest thing from pure white. *Her castle should be dark and smoldering as well,* Maleficent thought. She allowed herself a smile. She would see to that—soon.

But first she had other work to do. Spotting Udo trapped in a kite line, she swooped over to him. The sharp talons on her wings flashed as she sliced through the line, freeing him. Then she scanned the castle for any sign of Queen Ingrith. Her eyes were wild, blazing with fury and determination. Not spotting her prey, Maleficent flew lower. She picked up and flung aside soldiers who got in her way.

All she wanted was Ingrith.

To destroy her.

But where was she?

Arriving directly above the castle, Maleficent saw plumes of red dust emanating from the chapel. The smoke lifted into the sky, where it mingled with the clouds before fading from view. Maleficent also spotted dozens of faerie folk fleeing for their lives out the doors of the chapel. She saw Knotgrass attacking Gerda,

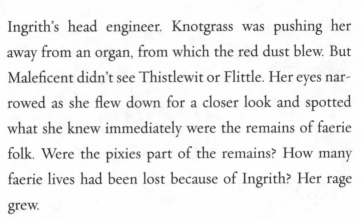

Ingrith's head engineer. Knotgrass was pushing her away from an organ, from which the red dust blew. But Maleficent didn't see Thistlewit or Flittle. Her eyes narrowed as she flew down for a closer look and spotted what she knew immediately were the remains of faerie folk. Were the pixies part of the remains? How many faerie lives had been lost because of Ingrith? Her rage grew.

Maleficent turned from the chapel. In the sky behind her she saw the warrior fey—what was left of them—coming toward her. She nodded. She would need their help if she was going to defeat Ingrith. She saw that now. The red dust was too powerful a weapon—even for her.

Phillip couldn't believe it had come to this. His wedding was a massacre. His mother was waging war on all the faeries. She had cursed his father. And now he was plummeting to the ground, clinging helplessly to a kite while one of his oldest and dearest friends clung to his feet.

The men thudded on the hard ground as they landed

and rolled free of the kite. Phillip was on his feet in an instant. He could see the chapel on the other side of the lawn. He had to get there—to Aurora and to the faerie folk. He ran.

But a moment later, Percival slammed into his back, knocking him to the ground once more. They rolled over the grass, pushing and shoving. Percival's arm pulled back and he moved to hit Phillip, but the prince slipped out of the way just in time. Jumping to his feet, he put his fists out in front of him. The two men shuffled back and forth, facing each other. If Phillip hadn't been so angry, he might have laughed. It reminded him so much of when they were boys, learning to wrestle while his father cheered them on. Then it had been for fun. Now it was for life.

"Yield!" Percival shouted, jumping forward and causing Phillip to take a quick step back.

Phillip kept moving as he shook his head. "My mother put the curse on the king so she could destroy the creatures of the Moors," Phillip said, trying to get through to his old friend. "Your men are paying heavily for it." As he spoke, another soldier shrieked as he fell from a Dark Fey's grasp. Percival's steps slowed and doubt crept into his eyes. Phillip opened his mouth to say more when suddenly there was a loud roar. Percival was knocked off his feet by a blur of wings and weathered tan skin.

All of a sudden, Phillip was staring at a Dark Fey. The first thing that flashed through his mind was Maleficent. The creature looked a lot like Aurora's godmother. He had the same wide wings and horns, but while Maleficent's were dark and her skin was pale and smooth, this fey had wings the color of sand and skin that was rough and worn.

It was Borra. The fey had fury in his eyes and rage in his heart. And his target was Phillip.

As Phillip watched, the fey's eyes narrowed. With a mighty flap of his wings, he swooped toward Phillip.

But just as the Dark Fey's hands were about to close around Phillip's throat, there was a shot and Borra fell to the ground. He lay there for a moment, a wound in his shoulder sizzling.

Looking over, Phillip saw Percival sitting up, a crossbow in his shaking hands. *Thank you,* Phillip mouthed, relief flooding over him.

But the feeling was short-lived. As Phillip watched in horror, Borra pushed himself to his feet. Stalking toward Percival, who scrambled backward in an attempt to get away, the Dark Fey leaned down and grabbed the crossbow from the human. He lifted it, then threw it to the ground, smashing it to pieces. Turning his attention once more to the human, Borra snarled and reached out a hand, ready to do the same thing to Percival that he had done to the crossbow.

Phillip's breathing was tense as he stood there, frozen. He couldn't wrap his head around any of it. His mother's betrayal. Her utter indifference to all the lives—human and faerie—that were ending.

His mother's insane desire was to destroy the Moors and every creature in them. *No,* he thought once more. His mother no longer made sense to him. Nor was she his family any longer, he realized. Family didn't hurt and destroy one another. Family didn't lie and betray.

Ingrith had stopped being his mother the moment she chose her vendetta over him and his father. His family was Aurora. Her happiness was his happiness. Her future was his future. And he would fight to his last breath to save both.

Percival's screams snapped Phillip back to the moment. Slowly, Phillip lifted his sword high above his head and stepped forward. He knew what he had to do. It was what he should have done long before. Distracted, Borra didn't notice Phillip as he walked over. He didn't notice him until Phillip pressed the tip of his sword to the Dark Fey's neck. Instantly, his flesh began to burn.

"Step away," Phillip ordered.

"Do it," Borra said, pressing his neck into the blade, impervious to the pain.

Percival looked up, surprise written all over his face. "Phillip," he started, "we're under attack!"

But Phillip shook his head. "This is not my fight," he said. "The queen wanted this war and you are giving it to her."

On the ground, Percival looked up at him, as if seeing Phillip for the first time. Phillip nodded at his friend. For too long he had been a silent witness to his mother's cruelty. He was done letting her ruin all that he found good. Once more, he turned and addressed Borra. "I will not allow her hate to ruin my kingdom or yours. I will have no fey blood on my hands." His words spoken, Phillip dropped the sword. It landed on the ground, bounced once, and then was still. In the fading light, the blade sparkled.

For a long, tense moment, the two men and one Dark Fey were still. Phillip kept his gaze locked on Borra as behind them a blast of magic shook the air. Finally, the fey gave the slightest of nods. He had come to kill Phillip, but now, begrudgingly, he found he could not. But that didn't mean others couldn't. With a flap of his mighty wings, he lifted into the air and flew toward the other Dark Fey.

Phillip sank to his knees. The breath he had been holding rushed out of him. He knelt there, his head

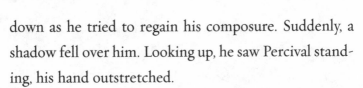

down as he tried to regain his composure. Suddenly, a shadow fell over him. Looking up, he saw Percival standing, his hand outstretched.

"My prince," Percival said.

Taking his hand, Phillip got to his feet. Percival didn't need to say more. His eyes said enough. The doubt he had had was gone. In its place were faith and trust. Percival, like Phillip, now knew the truth about Ingrith. And together, they were going to stop her. Once and for all.

CHAPTER EIGHTEEN

Maleficent heard the screams of terror from the soldiers below. She felt their fear as she sent wave after wave of magic to the ground. She smelled the fires that had begun to burn the grounds of Castle Ulstead. And it made her feel strong.

But there was another part of her, smaller and not as loud, that protested her reckless destruction. It sounded a lot like Conall, begging her to stop and think of what she was doing and who she was hurting.

She pushed that part down. It would do her no good when she finally found Ingrith. She needed rage to defeat the queen. Spotting a soldier out in the open, Maleficent dove and lifted him to her. As they hung in the air, the human's legs flailing helplessly, she glared at him. "Where is she?" she snarled.

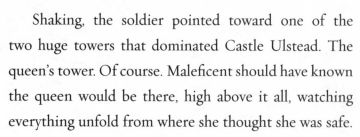

Shaking, the soldier pointed toward one of the two huge towers that dominated Castle Ulstead. The queen's tower. Of course. Maleficent should have known the queen would be there, high above it all, watching everything unfold from where she thought she was safe.

But she wasn't safe. Not any longer.

Dropping the soldier, Maleficent flew straight up the side of the tower. Fury burned in her eyes as she arrived at the top and spotted Queen Ingrith. The woman was standing in the center of the tower, arms at her sides, her face a mask of cold calm despite the chaos below. Soldiers guarded her, lining the edges, their weapons at the ready. Two huge catapults—armed with barrels of red dust—were aimed directly at Maleficent.

Maleficent wasn't afraid of the red dust or the death it would bring—so long as she could get to Ingrith first. Hovering in the air, she stared down the vile queen. Wind whipped at her dress and her hair, which had come loose, giving her a wilder, more evil look. What had filled the woman with such hate? Maleficent wondered.

It occurred to her, in a rather unappealing way, that she and the queen had that in common, at least. The hate. And the need for revenge. The only difference was Maleficent hadn't started this war. Ingrith had.

Dropping down to the opposite side of the tower, Maleficent kept her gaze locked on the queen. Two soldiers stepped between them. But with a swipe of her finger, Maleficent blew them aside. Now it was just the two of them.

Maleficent had had plenty of time in the Nest to think about the dinner and all that had transpired since then. She knew that Ingrith had used Maleficent's temper and reputation against her. The part that irked Maleficent was that she had let her vulnerability show. Her love for Aurora had weakened her. The thought made her anger stronger, and she lifted a hand, ready to strike Ingrith down with a wave of magic.

But the queen's words stopped her. "Killing me would be so easy," she said, gesturing to Maleficent's raised arm. "A wave of your hand and you get your revenge. Your kind is more predictable than humans."

In response, Maleficent's fangs flashed and her hand rose up. But a voice stopped her.

"Maleficent! No!"

Turning, Maleficent saw Aurora race out onto the tower. Her face was covered in dirt, her dress torn, but her eyes were as strong—and kind—as ever. Watching the pair, Ingrith smiled cruelly. "Well, almost as predictable."

Ignoring the cold woman, Aurora rushed over and put herself firmly between Maleficent and Ingrith. "I tried to make you be something you are not," she said softly, her eyes locked on Maleficent's.

Up close, Maleficent could now see pain in Aurora's eyes, too, as she begged for forgiveness.

"I'm forever sorry for that. But I know who you are and I know there is another way," Aurora said.

Maleficent raised one perfectly arched eyebrow. "You do not know me," she said. *You doubted me. You trusted* her *over me,* she almost added. But she bit back the bitter words. Conall's calm, kind voice echoed in her head, fighting with her own anger, weakening it. Hope, Conall had told her. She and Aurora had given him hope. He had believed in the power of Maleficent's love for Aurora over all things and he had ultimately sacrificed himself so they could be reunited. Could she let him die in vain?

Aurora, seeing the hesitation in Maleficent's eyes, slowly reached out her hand. "I do know you," she said. "You're my mother."

Maleficent's head snapped up. Her eyes locked on Aurora. *Mother.* The word echoed in her head, bouncing off moments and memories of Aurora as a baby, a young girl, and a young woman, happy and smiling. Aurora, reaching out and gently holding Maleficent's horn in her chubby hand. And then the word shifted, transformed, bouncing off newer memories. Memories of seeing the young fey learning to fly. She had spent so long believing she was a monster that she had almost failed to understand why Conall had put his faith in her. She wasn't the beast Ingrith said she was. She was a mother. A friend. A companion.

And, Maleficent thought, her mind made up, she was, and always would be, a protector.

Sensing the change in Maleficent, Ingrith reacted instantly. She lifted a huge crossbow in front of her. With her finger on the trigger, she smiled one more time, and then . . . she fired.

In a flash, a huge cloud of red dust hit Maleficent square in the chest. As the air exploded in red, Aurora screamed in anguish.

A moment later, the world in front of Maleficent vanished as she turned from fey to dust.

Aurora wept, her chest heaving as she watched the place where Maleficent had been. Now there was nothing but a cloud of dark dust that slowly began to dissipate in the wind.

Hearing the sound of footsteps above her, Aurora looked up. The simplest of movements was painful in light of what had just happened. Ingrith was peering down at her, a look of triumph on her face.

"Do you know what makes a great leader, Aurora?" Ingrith asked, unmoved by the tears that poured down Aurora's cheeks and onto the stones. "The ability to instill fear in your subjects—and then use that fear against your enemies." As she spoke, she waved her hand in the air, as though she could wave away the red dust that lingered. Aurora stared up at her, unable to find her voice or the strength to move.

Ingrith went on. "So, I told them the story about the evil witch, the princess she cursed, and how my son saved the beauty with True Love's Kiss."

Aurora's eyes widened. The woman was madder than she had thought. That wasn't the story. That was only *part* of the story. A twisted version that painted Maleficent a villain. Of course the people had hated the Dark Fey. They had trusted their queen to tell them the truth . . . and she had taken their trust and used it against them. She was, Aurora realized, pure evil. *She* was the witch, not Maleficent.

As if reading her thoughts, Ingrith nodded. "I know

you think I'm a monster," she continued. "But what I did to the king, to Maleficent, to my son . . . I did it for Ulstead." As she spoke, she took a step closer. Now her toes were nearly on top of Aurora's fingers. She stopped, inches away. "This," she finished, gesturing to the dust that had once been Maleficent, and then out at the devastation wrought by her war, "is *your* doing. You are a traitor to your kind—and you will pay for it."

Reaching down, Ingrith grabbed Aurora's wrist and yanked her painfully to her feet. Ignoring Aurora's protests, the queen dragged her closer to the edge of the tower. Aurora's feet scrambled on the stone. For such a fragile-looking woman, the queen was remarkably strong. Hate fueled her strength and clouded her mind. What else could explain what she was about to do? It was clear that Ingrith planned to send Aurora hurtling to her death while soldiers, fey, and even Phillip (who Aurora spotted on a neighboring parapet) watched.

The wind began to pick up as Aurora was dragged closer to the edge. The dust that had scattered all over the tower's stones lifted into the air and began to swirl.

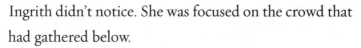

Ingrith didn't notice. She was focused on the crowd that had gathered below.

"Maleficent is dead!" she shouted.

From the human soldiers came muffled shouts of joy while the remaining fey gasped. Ingrith reveled in both reactions, her smile growing broader. "We will never again have to live in fear."

"Let go of me," Aurora said. Ingrith's words were making her sick. How could the woman be so happy in the face of such devastation? Aurora wrenched her arm back but Ingrith's grip was iron tight.

"Ulstead is free at last," Ingrith said triumphantly. But as her words drifted down and over the crowd, so, too, did more dust. It swirled in the air, shifting and transforming in front of her very eyes, slowly at first, then faster and faster as it grew and thickened.

"What's happening?" Aurora heard Ingrith ask. But she didn't look at the queen. Her eyes were glued to the dust.

Then the dust began to take shape. It wasn't clear at first. There seemed to be no rhyme or reason to the way it shifted and moved. But as Aurora watched, the dust that had once been Maleficent began pulling together and stretching until at last it became a massive phoenix.

Aurora gasped.

Maleficent had been transformed. Her love and the power of her sacrifice had tapped into the ancient being within her, so, like the mythical being of her ancestry, she was reborn.

Letting out a ferocious roar, the phoenix spread her wings. The bird turned, locking her eyes on Ingrith. The queen took an anxious step backward as she saw the look of death in the bird's eyes. Behind her, the soldiers dropped their weapons and scrambled away from the phoenix as green magic began to swell, casting the tower and the ground below in an eerie shadow.

Aurora looked at Maleficent—the phoenix—and a single tear trickled down her cheek. The bird was beautiful. She was wild and powerful, and despite the anger in her eyes, Aurora knew the bird represented everything good that had been in Maleficent's soul.

And then, before anything could be done to stop

her, Ingrith shoved Aurora over the ledge. With a cry, Aurora began to fall.

The wind rushed in her ears and whipped painfully at her cheeks. She saw the stones of the tower flashing by her as she plummeted toward the ground. Faster and faster she fell, her dress billowing around her as the clouds wafted teasingly at her from above. The ground rose, ready to meet her.

Then she heard it: over the wind, the cry of a bird and the flapping of powerful wings. A moment later, she felt the wings wrap around her, and then, with a thunderous crash, she—and Maleficent—slammed into the hard ground.

Aurora groaned. Her eyes, shut tightly, suddenly sprang open. There was precisely one thing on her mind: Maleficent!

Whipping her head around, Aurora saw that she was lying on the ground, cradled in the wings of the phoenix. As the majestic creature's wings opened, Aurora scrambled to her feet and moved a few steps away. Her eyes never left the phoenix. But the bird now lay motionless. The colorful wings did not move again. The eyes were closed.

Then, as she watched, the phoenix's eyes opened and she, too, rose. For a moment, the creature hovered in the air, an image from legend brought to beautiful life. Nearby, the Dark Fey who had survived bowed their heads in respect. And then, once more, the phoenix transformed. The wings became arms. The feathers turned black. And standing there, once again whole, was Maleficent. She was the same, yet different. Her eyes were filled with new wisdom and peace. And where she had once only had wings, now she had a tail, too—like the phoenix from which she had gained such strength.

With a cry of joy, Aurora raced to her mother. She flung her arms around Maleficent and clung to her, holding her like she would never let go. Maleficent hugged her right back. And then slowly, gently, Maleficent began to stroke Aurora's hair. "Beastie," she said softly.

Aurora let herself weep. For everything she'd almost lost. For all that Phillip *had* lost. For the darkness Ingrith had caused. But as the tears fell, they became tears of joy. She had gotten Maleficent back. Maleficent had come back for her. For love. Her mother might make light of it someday, but Aurora knew now, more than ever, that love was the most powerful magic of all.

Hearing footsteps, Aurora reluctantly pulled free. Phillip stepped forward, and this time it was his arms she fell into. As the Moor folk and the humans watched, they hugged. "What now?" Phillip asked, stepping out of the embrace.

Aurora looked from Phillip to Maleficent, and then out over the gathered crowd. They had seen such horror. What could possibly be done to fix the terror Ingrith's reign had brought upon them all? Then a smile began to spread over her face.

Taking a deep breath, she stepped toward the crowd. "Our two worlds will be united—right here, right now!" she declared.

Moving to stand beside her, Phillip nodded, a smile on his face. Aurora didn't need to say more. He knew what she was thinking, and with a strong voice, he added his support to her idea. "Let fear no longer divide us," he announced. "Today marks a new way forward—together!"

As faeries and humans began to cheer, Aurora looked over her shoulder at Maleficent. To her surprise, she saw Lickspittle coming up behind the Dark Fey. In his hands, he held the spindle. Aurora cocked her head, unsure of what was happening. Lickspittle had been Ingrith's pawn for so long. Was he there to hurt Maleficent—or help them in their new path forward?

"I believe this belongs to you," the pixie said, answering Aurora's unspoken question.

Reaching out, Maleficent took the object. In the light of day, it looked so harmless. The item had brought such sadness, yet in its own way, it had forged the path that had led them all here. This simple piece of wood had brought Aurora and Maleficent together; it had brought Aurora and Phillip together; and in a way, it would soon bring their kingdoms together.

"Curses never end," Lickspittle added as Maleficent stared down at the spindle. "They break."

Maleficent nodded. With a flick of her finger, she lifted the object into the air, where it hovered.

Below, Aurora addressed the crowd. "Today, there will be a wedding," she said. "It is not a union of two people, but a union of two kingdoms. All are invited. All are safe. *All* are welcome!"

As loud cheers filled the air, Maleficent let out a stream of green magic. It hit the spindle, shattering it into a thousand pieces. As it did, a shock wave of magic washed over the grounds of the castle. Flowers in the garden burst into bloom and butterflies swooped through the air as nature returned to Ulstead. In the middle of a gravel path, a huge willow tree shot up into the sky, its long, weeping branches drooping to the ground. The curse that had hung over so many for so long had finally ended.

Well, for most.

Hearing a shriek, Aurora turned and saw Ingrith being dragged out of the castle by the Dark Fey. The queen flailed and screamed, but her protests were in vain. Her clothes were ripped, her cheeks stained with dirt. Her usual composure was gone and panic was in its place. But no one stepped forward to save her.

"You cowards," she screeched. "We cannot live among monsters like these—"

Ingrith didn't get to say another word. Maleficent's fingers twitched and a ray of green magic blasted toward the queen. It faded with a puff of smoke and, standing where Ingrith once stood, was a goat. The animal let out a plaintive "baaa" and then sneezed.

Aurora stifled a laugh. There could be no worse punishment for the queen who hated nature than to spend the rest of her days trapped as a goat.

"Someone should really cover her horns," Maleficent said, meeting Aurora's gaze. Then she flashed a smile— fangs and all. Aurora laughed and the sound broke any remaining tension between them. The curse was truly broken. It was time for a celebration.

CHAPTER NINETEEN

WHEN AURORA ANNOUNCED THAT SHE AND PHILLIP WERE GOING TO GET MARRIED THEN AND THERE— SHE HADN'T ENTIRELY THOUGHT IT THROUGH. Now, as she stood protected from the eyes of the gathered crowd by the leaves of the willow tree, she momentarily regretted her impulsivity. While she'd never been one to be particularly vain, the idea of getting married to Phillip in a dress that was ripped, torn, and covered in filth was . . . disappointing.

Aurora turned at the sound of rustling leaves and saw Maleficent entering the canopy. "How do I look?" Aurora asked, trying to sound happy as she tucked a loose strand of hair behind her ear.

Maleficent's eyes narrowed and a frown tugged at her lips.

Not good, I guess, Aurora thought.

But before Aurora could make any excuses, Maleficent flicked a long finger and magic washed over Aurora. When it cleared, Aurora's hair was smooth and her face was clean. A new dress had replaced the tattered one she'd been wearing. And unlike the heavy, severe dress Ingrith had given her, this dress was breezy and light and allowed her to move freely. Covered in fragile pink flowers, its train billowed out behind Aurora like a lace river. The bodice was made of the purest white silk and the fabric of the thin sleeves was nearly translucent. The skirt of the dress flowed out from Aurora's hips, covered the ground at her feet, and made it seem as though she and the dress were part of the same ground. It was strong, yet fragile. Bold, yet timeless. It was the embodiment of Aurora and the Moors themselves.

Looking over at Maleficent, Aurora clapped her hands. "It's beautiful," she breathed. "Thank you."

For a moment, mother and daughter stood quietly. The air felt heavy with emotion. There were so many things Aurora wanted to say. Apologies for what she had done and how she had acted, promises for the future. But it felt like the wrong time. Those words didn't need to be spoken. She knew Maleficent had forgiven her. Instead, she posed a very important question.

"Will you walk me down the aisle?" Aurora asked.

There was a pause.

"You know, they say it is bad luck to deny a bride on her wedding day," Aurora added.

Ever so slowly, a grin spread across Maleficent's face. "Very well. If you insist."

As relief—and happiness—washed over Aurora, she peeked out at the castle through the willow's branches. Like her, it seemed lighter, happier, and the feeling of hope began to grow. And as she spotted someone emerging from the castle doors, the hope grew. It was the king! The spindle's destruction had awoken him. He was dazed but okay.

While Phillip ran to him, Aurora turned back to Maleficent. The day had been full of heartbreak. But things were changing. The spindle was destroyed.

Ingrith was gone. The king was awake. Maleficent was alive and well. It was time to look to the future. It was time for a wedding.

As the setting sun filled the sky with a riot of colors, Aurora stood at the end of a long makeshift aisle in the middle of Castle Ulstead's lawn. Beautiful flowers lined her path, draping the ground in petals and filling the air with their perfume. Firefly faeries flitted above, creating a twinkle of lights to brighten her way. On either side, more faeries stood intermingled with humans, at ease and at peace as they waited for Aurora.

Aurora thought her heart might burst as she looked out at the guests and farther along to where Phillip stood beside Diaval. She smiled as she saw King John approach and embrace his son. He whispered something into Phillip's ear and then, with a happy smile, stepped back, allowing his son the place of honor at the head of the aisle. A moment later, Ingrith, in her goat form, skipped in front of the men. At this, Aurora's smile faltered only slightly. While it was bittersweet for them to see Ingrith this way, she knew that neither Phillip, nor his father, truly minded the outcome. Aurora shook her head. Now was not the time to dwell on the sad moments or the lives lost. She had imagined this day for so long. And now it was here. And it was better than anything her dreams could have conjured.

Maleficent's eyes were full of emotion as she stood beside Aurora. Aurora squeezed her mother's hand, and the music began to play. Together, they walked down the long aisle. Stopping in front of Phillip and King John, Maleficent gazed at Aurora. Aurora didn't need words to know what her mother was thinking. She could feel her love. As Maleficent gently placed Aurora's hand in Phillip's, Aurora knew the faerie was giving her a mother's blessing.

"The rings, please," the officiant said.

Pinto stepped forward. The hedgehog faerie's face was aglow with pride as she held up two rings. Made of vines, the rings were simple but stronger than metal.

They, like the moors from where they had come, would last forever. With a satisfied nod, Maleficent stepped aside and took her place next to Diaval.

Aurora turned her attention to the officiant, but not before she heard Diaval say, "I like the new look. And I was thinking—"

"Nasty habit," Maleficent said in her cool, even voice. "You should stop."

Diaval ignored the Dark Fey's snarky retort and pushed on. "I was *thinking* that we do the bear thing from now on. I think we would look good together, prowling the Moors—"

"I don't prowl," Maleficent said, stopping Diaval mid-sentence.

Then she waved her hand in the direction of Arabella, Ingrith's horrid cat, and the creature transformed into a beautiful young woman. Diaval gasped as Arabella's eyes locked on his. "This is good, too," he said.

Focusing on the officiant, Aurora listened as he spoke of love and honor. He asked them to promise to cherish the good and be patient through the bad. Aurora

and Phillip had indeed lived through enough bad for a lifetime. It was time to get to the happily ever after.

"Do you, Phillip, take Aurora to be—"

Phillip didn't let the officiant finish before answering, "I do."

"I do, too!" Aurora said, just as eagerly.

The officiant laughed. "Okay, you may kiss—"

But again the couple didn't let him finish. Their lips met, and they melted into each other in a kiss that was completely magical. It was a kiss that symbolized their love and marriage but also defined their future—and the future of their kingdoms. For all those who were gathered, it was clear the future would be wonderful.

EPILOGUE

So the days passed and the seasons changed—as did Castle Ulstead. With Queen Ingrith gone, the palace became brighter. The hallways filled with laughter. The coldness ebbed, and warmth entered. Bright flowers bloomed in the gardens and within the castle walls. It was a stark contrast to Ingrith's reign and her harsh, taxidermic decor. Despite its massive size, Castle Ulstead became a home.

At the heart of this new home were Aurora and Phillip. Their marriage had brought the peace they had promised and finally united the citizens of both kingdoms. Human children of Ulstead and faerie children of the Moors played alongside one another, their laughter a joyful reminder of how far things had come. In uniting their kingdoms, Aurora and Phillip had created a better one, a place where all were welcome.

Standing on a balcony, Aurora looked out over her kingdom. A gentle spring breeze carried the smell of impending summer, and on the grounds far below, she could see flowers blooming. Beyond the river, the Moors looked lush and rich as leaves and flowers flourished. Hearing footsteps, she smiled as Phillip joined her on the balcony.

"What is it, love?" he asked, taking her hand.

Aurora grinned. "It's a new day," she said simply.

"I suppose it is," Phillip answered.

As they watched, Maleficent appeared and hovered over the balcony.

In the days since their wedding, the Dark Fey had grown more comfortable around Phillip and even King John. She spent equal time between Castle Ulstead and the Moors to show all that the peace between the kingdoms was true and lasting.

But the time had come for Maleficent to return to the Moors more permanently. The faeries needed her—especially the Dark Fey who now called the Moors home. While they flourished in the openness the Nest had never offered, they lacked guidance without Conall. Maleficent had become their de facto leader—and mother. While Aurora would miss the undivided attention, she knew soon enough there would be reason for Maleficent to visit Ulstead.

"Maleficent," Phillip said in greeting, unaware of his wife's thoughts.

"Could you stay awhile?" Aurora couldn't help asking, her voice a bit shaky. She knew she sounded every bit the young girl she had once been, but she didn't care. She was going to miss her mother, even if she was only across the river.

Maleficent smiled at Aurora. Taking her hand, she squeezed it gently. "I have work to do," she said.

Aurora nodded. Maleficent was right. In the days following the wedding, Maleficent had told her all about the Nest and Conall. Aurora had wept when she had learned Maleficent had lost such a wonderful friend. But she also heard the happiness in her voice and saw

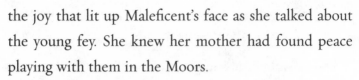

the joy that lit up Maleficent's face as she talked about the young fey. She knew her mother had found peace playing with them in the Moors.

She also knew that Maleficent would always be there. Together, they had made that possible. The division between the kingdoms was gone, once and for all. Both the Moors and Ulstead were flourishing. And as her mother moved to fly away, Aurora knew there was another reason for them to remain forever connected.

Maleficent turned and looked at Aurora and Phillip over her shoulder. "I'll see you at the christening," she said, smiling.

With a flap of her wings, Maleficent soared into the sky. Behind her, Aurora laughed as Phillip turned to her in surprise—her secret revealed. As he pulled her into a hug, Aurora watched Maleficent fly toward the Moors, her wings spread wide. As she dove, a group of young fey flew up to meet her. Even from where she stood, Aurora could hear their laughter as they called to Maleficent, asking her to play.

Aurora smiled. Her family was growing. And so, it seemed, was Maleficent's. Individually, they had found happiness they didn't know was possible. But together, they had made dreams come true. Together, they'd created a world where there would be love—forever and always.